"I WANT TO REPO

Chief Allie Voegl[e...] quick "am I deali[ng...] recovered and asked professionally. Whose murder?"

"Dick Obey," she replied.

He shot back: "No! You can't report Dick Obey's murder. I have the Delaware County coroner's report. Dick Obey fell drunk into a ditch and was killed by a pack of dogs."

"I want to see the crime scene photos. Do you have them?"

He exploded, "Of course not. Why the hell would I need to look at them? Besides, there are no *crime* scene photos. It was an accident. Look, why don't you stick to cows and I'll take care of crime?"

"Believe me. I can see things you can't," she said gently.

"Yeah, I suppose you can read a lot of things in a field of manure."

She ignored the provocation. "I'm trained in something that is very close to forensic medicine. I investigate 'crimes' against animals all the time. The perpetrators may be bacteria or viruses or allergies or cruel masters—but the investigative method is the same."

Dr. Nightingale
Comes Home

A DEIDRE QUINN
NIGHTINGALE
MYSTERY

Lydia Adamson

A SIGNET BOOK

SIGNET
Published by the Penguin Group
Penguin Books USA Inc., 375 Hudson Street,
New York, New York 10014, U.S.A.
Penguin Books Ltd, 27 Wrights Lane,
London W8 5TZ, England
Penguin Books Australia Ltd, Ringwood,
Victoria, Australia
Penguin Books Canada Ltd, 10 Alcorn Avenue,
Toronto, Ontario, Canada M4V 3B2
Penguin Books (N.Z.) Ltd, 182–190 Wairau Road,
Auckland 10, New Zealand

Penguin Books Ltd, Registered Offices:
Harmondsworth, Middlesex, England

First published by Signet, an imprint of Dutton Signet,
a division of Penguin Books USA Inc.

First Printing, February, 1994
10 9 8 7 6 5 4 3 2 1

 REGISTERED TRADEMARK—MARCA REGISTRADA

Printed in the United States of America

PUBLISHER'S NOTE
This is a work of fiction. Names, characters, places, and incidents either
are the product of the author's imagination or are used fictitiously, and
any resemblance to actual persons, living or dead, events, or locales is
entirely coincidental.

Chapter One

The country road was empty. It was six in the morning. A dull gray spring morning. The red jeep bounced merrily along. On the stereo deck was Patsy Cline singing "I Fall to Pieces." Deirdre Quinn Nightingale had both hands on the wheel, one hand tapping time to the music with one finger. Charlie Gravis sat next to her, his head slumped, his eyes closed.

Didi, as she was called, felt very good. Howard Danto had called the night before and asked her to come over. He had some problems with his goat herd. And Howard Danto was one of the "new money" breeders and farmers in the town of Hillsbrook, Dutchess County, New York. It was the first time since Didi had returned home to open a veterinary practice a year ago that one of these new money people had called for her services.

Most of her clients in the past year had been old-line, struggling dairy farmers who had known her mother and Didi as a child. She loved them all dearly, but they didn't pay their bills and were extremely cynical toward the entire science of veterinary medicine. Oh, they used state-of-the-art milking machinery and computer-generated feed mixes . . . and when they were ill, the humans, they availed themselves of the latest in diagnostic and surgical techniques.

But when it came to one of their cows, they had the fatalism of fifteenth-century bedouins.

Danto would be different—she just knew it. She had heard he was interested in making the best soft goat cheese in the world and that he would pay anything to accomplish this. Sure, dairy cow operations were what a rural vet was all about in New York State; and this was what Didi wanted to do and she was happy—but she needed to expand her practice, both financially and intellectually. Howard Danto would be a beginning. After Danto might come one of those new thoroughbred horse-breeding operations which had recently arrived in the county. Didi smiled, almost longingly. She could visualize herself entering one of those beautiful, enormous, wood-paneled stables—twenty yearlings all in a row, waiting for her . . . multimillion-dollar babies sired by Seattle Slew and Alydar and Danzig and Mr. Prospector. Yes, she felt good.

"Could you lower it a bit, Miss Quinn?" Charlie Gravis asked.

"I thought you were asleep, Charlie," Didi said breezily, making no effort to lower the volume of Patsy Cline.

"Hard to sleep with this racket, Miss Quinn," Charlie replied, now staring out of the window and shaking his head slowly as if it were impossible to truly explain things to such a difficult young woman. He always called her by her mother's maiden name.

Didi kept driving. Should she lower the volume or not? If one gave Charlie an inch, he took a yard. A yard, he took half the circumference of the earth. Old Charlie Gravis was a problem. She had inherited the seventy-one-year-old man from her mother along with three other rural people who had lived and worked on her mother's estate (if one could call it that) for years. When her mother died and Didi returned home, she simply didn't know what to do with them. They weren't paid salaries—just room and board. And they kept the place in order, after a fashion. So Didi had kept them on, as a sign of respect to her mother's memory. And she had made Charlie Gravis her veterinary assistant.

In retrospect, it had been a mistake. These retainers did exactly as they pleased. They kept a small herd of hogs for meat even though Didi didn't want hogs slaughtered on the premises. They took potshots at woodchuck and deer even though Didi told them not to. Yes, they

7

were a problem—Charlie Gravis, Mrs. Tunney, Abigail, and Trent Tucker.

As for Charlie as a veterinary assistant: well, he was still strong and dependable in many ways, but he considered himself the dean of natural healers in the county. He had a herbal remedy for every animal disorder from distemper to bee bite to foot rot, and he would regale her clients at the drop of a hat.

I must be logical, Didi thought. I must not let Charlie Gravis irritate me. I must think it out. Is the music too loud? If too loud, then turn it down. Didi contemplated the problem as the jeep sped along. She was sorry now she didn't get a chance for her breathing exercises before she left the house. Yoga in the early morning in the great outdoors always helped her meet the Charlie Gravis problems with ease. But there had been no time. She had to be at Howard Danto's place on time, not only because she wanted to make a good impression on him, professionally, but because at eight o'clock in the morning she had to be at the Hillsbrook Diner to chair the local Committee on Rabies Control. She had to keep to schedule.

Didi looked over once at Charlie Gravis, sighed, and then leaned forward to turn the music down.

It was at this precise moment that the jeep hit one of those mud holes which have made

Upper Dutchess County, New York the broken axle capital of the civilized world. The sturdy country road seemed to just give way and the jeep plunged crazily into a pit of moldering mud . . . bouncing the occupants around like coconuts. Five seconds later they were through it, unhurt, on firm ground again.

The problem was, since it was a nice morning, Didi had kept the side flaps of the jeep open, and now both of them and the inside as well as the outside of the vehicle were covered with clumpy reddish mud. It had splattered all over them.

Didi pulled the jeep over to the side of the road to recover. She stared, or rather glared at Charlie Gravis, as if the whole thing were his fault. Then she burst out laughing.

Was she as covered with mud as Charlie? He looked like The Swamp Thing.

Five minutes later, cleaned up to the best of their ability, Didi and Charlie drove through the front gate of the Howard Danto farm.

The proprietor was waiting for them where the driveway ended. He was a huge man, in his late thirties, with an uncanny resemblance to the singer Burl Ives. He cradled a thermos in his meaty hand and the moment they stepped out of the jeep and introduced themselves to him, he poured them some coffee into paper cups. Didi was enchanted. Danto confirmed the old adage that while dairy farmers always dressed like dairy farmers, so-called gentleman farmers always dressed like crazy dairy farmers. It wasn't cold, but he had two mufflers around his neck and the most ragged pair of coveralls Didi had ever seen, over a bright red sweatshirt on which was printed PROPERTY OF SAN QUENTIN PRISON.

"Something very strange is happening to my goats," he said with genuine concern, an almost motherly pain in his voice.

"Well, let's take a look at them," Didi replied in her best professional manner, crumpling her paper cup and flinging it into the back of the jeep.

Off they trudged, Danto and Didi side by side, Charlie Gravis in the rear, carrying Didi's veterinary bag and the large notebook that she used to record her thoughts on examination and treatment . . . Charlie playing the role of scribe.

As they walked, Howard Danto began to tell his story: how he had moved to the country after being a stockbroker in New York. And he began to outline his dream: How he was going to produce and market the finest soft goat cheese in the world from the finest goat's milk. He extolled the high, uniformly distributed butterfat content in his herd's milk. How he fed them no hay or prepared food . . . only forage all year long—brush, small trees, weeds, broadleaf plants—plus oats and corn and just a dollop of high protein calf supplement for extra minerals and vitamins. How he had constructed various forage plots that could be closed off easily by strong, portable fences when a given area was overgrazed.

Didi smiled as she heard Charlie Gravis groan behind her. Old dairy farmers like him had nothing but bewildered contempt for wealthy gentleman-farmer visionaries like Danto. Didi appreciated Charlie's skepticism but she loved people like Danto, as much as she loved old dairy farmers who struggled so hard and so long in a no-win situation.

They passed the goat sheds and the milking stands and Danto pointed out the low green and white building in the distance which he called, with obvious pride, his "cheese factory."

Then they reached the herd. Didi immediately identified them as French Alpines—erect ears, long heads, straight or slightly dished noses. And the wide variety of colors was there—brown and white, black and white, solids. It wasn't a small herd either; more than twenty, mostly does with a scattering of kids and a buck or two.

Didi felt a surge of well-being as she contemplated the goats foraging around her. The wisdom of her decision to return home, assume the responsibility of her mother's property rather than sell it, and become an old-fashioned rural vet (if Dutchess County could still be characterized as rural) was apparent to her. After graduating from veterinary school at the University of Pennsylvania, she had done a year's postgraduate work in India, of all places—half because she loved elephants dearly and half because she had to recover far away from the scene of a very unhappy love affair. When she returned to the U.S., she had a series of short-lived staff positions at large suburban dog and cat hospitals and posh equine centers that featured swimming pool therapy and sophisticated surgical and laser techniques for mending broken-down racehorses. She was unhappy at all of them, dreadfully.

"My goats are butting each other," Danto whispered, as if it were terribly illicit erotic behavior. "Suddenly, for no reason, they butt each other, or me, or the side of a building, or a fence post."

"Well, Mr. Danto," Didi explained, "goats have a pecking order, like chickens. They will butt in the sheds, for example, to get their feed first."

"No," Danto replied, his voice rising, "not in the sheds. In the fields. There's plenty of food around for everyone. No, it's not that. Look, come over to Laura."

They walked over to Laura, a refined-looking doe, who was calmly and methodically stripping a low lying shrub.

Laura seemed to ignore them. Didi studied

her. She looked very much the healthy French Alpine, a wide-backed milking doe with firm, good-colored udders, not too low slung.

"Just wait, just wait," Howard Danto said, speaking softly. "Any little bit of extra stress will get her going."

Laura had, at first, appeared unconcerned with the presence of strangers, but now she stopped feeding and stared curiously. Then she took a few steps. Then she stopped.

"Wait," Danto kept whispering, "and watch for it."

As if on cue, Laura shot forward and slammed her lovely head against Charlie Gravis's thigh. Charlie cursed and, with an instinctual old dairyman's response, smacked his hand hard against the doe's rump, knocking her sideways. Danto uttered a moan of psychic pain at lovely Laura's getting hit. Didi glared at Charlie reproachfully.

Danto recovered. "There, do you see? They all do it now. All of them, even the kids. And they all have welts on their sides to prove it."

Didi realized that it was, indeed, very strange goat behavior—not a butt front on but more of a side head slam.

Her experience with goats was not extensive, but she knew the drill. She knew exactly what questions the examination had to answer. Vet school had indelibly imprinted them onto her brain.

Approaching Laura, with Charlie and Danto surrounding the doe to keep her steady, Didi commenced the hands-on examination while at the same time eliciting information from Howard Danto.

Is Laura alert and inquisitive? Is Laura's appetite constant? Is she chewing her cud? Are her eyes bright, without discharge? Is her nose dry and cool? Is her coat clean and glossy? Any abscesses under the jaw? On the legs? Are her droppings firm and pelleted? Is her urine light brown—without traces of blood? Is her breathing regular? Is her gait steady? Is she favoring any one of her feet? Any changes in quantity or quality of milk yield? Any stringiness in her milk? Any undue sensitivity in her udders?

Didi stepped back. According to the textbook, this goat was healthy. She caught a glimpse of her watch. It was seven fifteen. She had to be at that meeting. But she also had to do a good job for Howard Danto. She stared at the goat. Laura seemed unconcerned once again, going back to her bush. But she was making some sounds: bleating quietly, almost a whisper.

"What do you think?" Danto asked, ever anxious.

"I don't know yet. She appears to be healthy," Didi replied. Danto shook his head sadly.

Didi remembered what her favorite professor, Hiram Bechtold, used to say over and over again: "In most animal work, symptoms are clinically meaningless—unless you don't know what the hell to do."

Didi grimaced. Her mind went back to the symptom—head slamming. It signified nothing to her.

But head *pressing* did. Had Laura really wanted to head press rather than head slam? If so, it could be CCN. That was always a possibility.

"Do they ever keep their heads pressed for a while against a hard object or another goat?" she asked.

"No," Danto replied.

"Have you noticed any sign of failing eyesight?"

"No."

"Are you sure?"

"Well, the kids stumble a bit. But . . ."

"You see, Mr. Danto, it could be CCN."

"What's that?" Danto asked eagerly.

"Cerebral Cortico Necrosis," Didi answered.

"Can it be cured?"

"Oh, easily. It's just a fancy term for thiamine deficiency. It's caused by a fungus that destroys the ability of the enzymes to produce thiamine. But there's a problem here. You see, the fungus is ingested with their feed. And nowadays, the fungus, for the most part, is found in hay. Yet you said you don't give your goats any hay whatsoever."

"No, I definitely don't feed them hay—any

15

kind of hay," Danto said, obviously disappointed that it wasn't such an easily treatable disorder.

Didi realized what she should do next—just take a whole lot of blood and stool samples from the goats and send them off to a lab. But she wanted to impress Danto now. She didn't want to do that tired vet thing. She wanted to show Danto that, while she might be young and relatively inexperienced and female, she had a better diagnostic grasp of goats than any other damn vet in the county—particularly the middle-aged, lab-obsessed males.

"Of course, it could be listeriosis," she mused out loud.

"What's that?" Danto asked, grasping for curable straws.

"It's also called circling disease. The goats head-press first, then start acting funny, and then just begin to circle. It comes from a bacteria in the soil ingested through the goat's mouth or via an eye infection."

"Is it bad?" Danto asked.

"Sometimes . . . but if you catch it early, antibiotics do the trick."

"These goats ain't circling," Charlie said. He always had to put his two cents in, Didi thought. But he was right. And Danto agreed.

Didi squatted on the ground like an Indian, folded her hands pensively in front of her, and watched Laura browse. She blocked out Danto and Charlie and the time and the weather. She studied Laura carefully for about three minutes from her squatting position, then stood and approached the goat.

"What a lovely goat you are, Miss Laura," Didi whispered in a playful manner and slowly began to scratch the top of the doe's head. French Alpine goats are exquisite, Didi mused—perfectly proportioned, a bit haughty, a bit inquisitive.

"Are you going to tell me what's bothering you, Miss Laura, or make me find out for myself?" she cooed into one of Laura's lovely erect ears. All Laura uttered in response was an indecipherable bleat—almost a whisper.

Didi kept watching her. It was obvious that Laura was experiencing some kind of discomfort—intermittently. But, Didi reasoned, it could not be pain. She was just too placid between bouts. And goats in pain often vented their aggression against themselves or went into isolation. No, it wasn't pain.

Didi scratched Laura's chest this time, staring into the goat's eyes. "Now, Miss Laura, I don't give a damn if you are the best milking goat in all of Dutchess County. If you don't tell me what's ailing you, I'm going to . . ."

It was decidedly unprofessional behavior from a vet trained at that temple of scientific veterinary medicine, the University of Pennsylvania, but it somehow worked. Didi broke off her sentence halfway through, stared incredulously at her own scratching hand, then let out a whoop that spooked poor Laura.

Turning to Danto, she called out: "Of course! Laura has an itch! She has an itch she can't get to. So she and the other goats slam their heads because it's an itch within. It has to be inside the ears!"

Then Didi turned to Charlie, who was standing with the notebook closed, obviously having once again forgotten to take notes. She ignored his incompetence. "Charlie! Go to the jeep and bring me back the microscope. It's buried somewhere in the back, in a wooden case." Charlie gave her an "is this really necessary?" look, then trudged off.

She waited with Danto in silence. She looked much younger than her twenty-eight years—small and thin with short black hair, bangs, and very pale green eyes. "Pretty as a picture" everyone had always said about her. She was wearing overalls with crisscross straps, a Greenpeace Save The Whales sweatshirt with a hood, and a pair of enormous rubber mud boots with the tops turned down.

Charlie finally returned, puffing and lugging the case. "Do me a favor, Charlie. Set the scope up on the case and take out the slides and the solution."

Didi removed long-stem cotton swabs from

her leather satchel and signaled to Danto that he should hold the goat.

She waited until Danto was holding Laura still, then swabbed deep into her left ear.

She walked to the case on which the battered microscope now sat; rolled the swab onto one of the slides; fixed it with a drop of solution and slid it under the lens.

Didi squatted close to the ground for a full minute, looking into the scope. Then she stood up, grinning, and said to Danto: "Take a look."

The large man had to be helped into a squatting position and supported while he gazed at the slide.

"My God!" he exclaimed. "They have legs!"

Didi laughed and helped him up. "Yes," she said, "they sure do. They are mites. Your goats are infected with Psoroptic Mange."

Howard Danto's face turned ashen. "That's fatal, isn't it?" he whispered.

Didi shook her head vigorously. "No! No! You're thinking of Sarcoptic Mange. That's deadly and ugly. No, this kind of mange can be quickly cleared up with any one of a dozen commercial washes. Just squirt it in the ears using one of those rubber syringes, like people use for earwax."

Danto heaved a sigh of relief. He wiped his enormous face with a small checked handkerchief.

Didi looked at her watch. It was ten minutes to eight. Even if she left immediately, she would still be late for the meeting. But, if she drove back to her place, picked up the medication, and brought it back to Danto—she would be very, very late and probably would have to miss the meeting altogether. It was a problem; she wanted very much to help Danto administer the wash the first time.

Her thoughts raced. It wasn't an important meeting. She had been named coordinator of the antirabies effort in the area by the director of the County Agricultural Extension Service, mainly because none of the other vets were willing. There wasn't much anyone could do really—the rabies epidemic was now in its fifth year. If the people didn't realize that they had to cover their garbage, report crazed raccoons, and leash their dogs, then no amount of meetings would help. But if she didn't show up, she'd miss talking to Dick Obey, probably her only real friend in the town. He was a wonderful and wise dairy farmer whose operation had gone bust in 1989, whose wife had died of cancer in 1985, and whose son had been killed in Vietnam in 1970. He still clung to his land, doing all sorts of odd jobs. It was Dick Obey who had made sure that farmers in the area used her as a vet when she first hung out her shingle. He never admitted to that, but she knew it was true. After the meetings in the diner, Didi and Obey always went into town together and talked about a million things. It

was an interlude both always looked forward to
. . . it was the real reason they both showed up
for the meetings religiously. No, she had to get
to the meeting.

"Look, Mr. Danto, I have an appointment at
the Hillsbrook Diner that I just can't break. My
assistant, Charlie, is going to drop me off there,
then pick up the ear wash, and come back here.
He'll help you administer it."

"That's fine . . . that's okay," Howard Danto
said. "I'm much obliged for what you have
done. Obliged and grateful."

"Do you understand, Charlie?" Didi asked.
Charlie Gravis nodded his grizzled head.

Danto walked them back to the jeep, reiterat-
ing over and over again his gratitude. They
shook hands finally and the red jeep moved off.

"Do you understand, Charlie? I'll get out at
the Hillsbrook Diner. You take the jeep, go
back to the house, get the wash, and deliver it
to Danto. Help him with the goats." She
handed Charlie a slip of paper with the name
of the substance that had to be delivered. "Take
a couple of rubber syringes and just show him
how to do it."

Charlie seemed to scrunch down in his seat.
"You know, Miss Quinn," he said, "a strong hot
vinegar wash with a few garlic cloves would do
just as well."

"Damn it, Charlie! Follow my instructions!"
Didi responded angrily. This was one client that

Didi didn't want corrupted by Charlie's herbal wisdom.

"You're the boss," Charlie said.

"I guess I am."

At 8:20, the red jeep pulled off the road in front of the Hillsbrook Diner. Didi ran out of the vehicle, into the diner, through the front area, and into the back room, which had since time immemorial been a popular community meeting place.

Several tables had been pushed together. The committee was waiting for her. There was John Theobold, dairy farmer from Long Road; Roger Brice, dairy farmer from Spindle Road, right across from Didi's land; Frank Draper, owner of the most successful organic farm in Dutchess County, whose clients were some of the poshest restaurants in Manhattan; and George Hammond, the county agent.

"It's about time," said Frank Draper. Didi apologized for being late but her eyes were searching for Dick Obey.

He wasn't there. The chair he usually sat in, dozing, near the wall, was occupied. But not by Dick Obey. By a New York State Trooper in full regalia . . . wide hat . . . leather holster and belt . . . creased uniform . . . shoulder strap . . . shining boots.

"Well, damn it, tell her," she heard John Theobold instruct the trooper.

He removed his elegant, wide-brimmed hat

and stared at Didi Quinn Nightingale. "Mr. Obey was found this morning. On Route Twenty-eight, outside Delhi, in Delaware County. He had been drinking heavily and fell onto the side of the road. A pack of stray dogs must have found him there, unconscious. We discovered the body just as it got light. He was dead. His jugular ripped out. The dogs must have gone berserk."

Didi sat down slowly, very slowly, onto a chair. She could not believe what she was hearing. Someone brought her a cup of coffee with a spoon.

Chapter Two

"That girl is going to get pneumonia," Charlie Gravis said, staring out the kitchen window at Didi, who was doing her yogic breathing exercises in the lotus position in the yard near the hog shed. There was a cold wind blowing across the property. The morning was overcast. It did not seem like spring.

"Leave her be," Mrs. Tunney said. "She is grieving." Mrs. Tunney was wearing a ragged yellow bathrobe over her clothes. She was stirring an enormous pot of oatmeal.

Abigail sat quietly at the large, slate-topped kitchen table, waiting patiently for breakfast. Her golden hair was piled up on her head. She was thin, almost emaciated, with translucent skin, and she wore an old red sweater over a matched pair of sweats.

Across from her sat Trent Tucker. He was impatient to get on with his chores. Trent was nineteen, eight years younger than Abigail but, unlike Abigail, paid no heed whatsoever to what either Mrs. Tunney or Charlie Gravis said. All four were vaguely related: distant cousins whose bloodlines were dimmed in the early history of Dutchess County. How they had all ended up together under Didi's mother's tender care was a chain of complex coincidences that could only happen in dairy cow country.

"The girl needs a husband," Mrs. Tunney said, continuing to stir the pot with great authority. The steam was rising.

"She sure needs something," Charlie Gravis agreed. He stared out the window, past the young woman holding her breath in the lotus position. He could see a flurry of whitetail deer near the pine forest—one of the largest remaining stands of virgin white pine in the county. It had been Didi's mother's pride and joy. "She's been in a fog since Dick Obey died," he continued, "and it's more than two weeks already."

"The last one you tried to fix her up with was almost seventy years old," Trent Tucker said, winking at Abigail.

"But he was healthy. As strong as an ox," the sixty-six-year-old Mrs. Tunney said. "And that is what that young woman needs . . . a healthy, stable man. Then she wouldn't be doing that nonsense in the yard."

Having made that pronouncement, she lifted the pot to the table and filled the bowls. Milk, honey, and bread accompanied the hot cereal.

It was a huge kitchen that divided the early nineteenth-century stone house. North of the kitchen was the main dining room, sitting room, library, and, upstairs, the three bedrooms, one of which was occupied by Didi. South of the kitchen was the added-on "servants" quarters where Charlie Gravis, Mrs. Tunney, Abigail, and Trent Tucker lived, each to his or her own drafty cubicle. Past their rooms was another addition to the house, which had originally been storeroom and now functioned as Didi's small animal clinic, which was open two days a week in the late afternoon.

Everything in the enormous kitchen was dramatically unmodern, particularly the ancient behemoth of a refrigerator that made unbelievable noises twenty-four hours a day. The closets and pantry and counters were of splintering wood. The whitewashed walls of the kitchen were without paintings or decoration of any kind.

Only one object, hanging boldly from the ceiling by a rope and spike, could be considered decorative, if one had a sense of humor. It was a large brass bird cage, the largest in Dutchess County, perhaps in the entire state of New York. Once it had housed Didi's mother's beloved gray parrots. Faith Quinn Nightingale had, of course, named them Hope and Charity. Both had died before their mistress died, and only Faith had mourned for them. They were very fractious birds.

Surrounding the table, watching the four people breakfast, was an assortment of dogs and cats, all of whom lived along the outside perimeter of the house; the cats in the foundation; the dogs under the four sets of stone steps. They were all allowed free entry to the house when they wished, if they could get in, and they always managed to show up for breakfast because Abigail was extremely generous with bread crusts.

When Didi finished her breathing exercises that morning and walked into the kitchen, no one said a word. They kept on eating oatmeal.

Didi walked past the table, picked up a piece of bread, and went to the refrigerator. She opened the massive door and dug her hand into a paper bag full of Granny Smith apples. She felt awkward as usual when around all of them. She just never knew how to speak to them . . . how to greet them . . . how to deal with them. It was all so confusing. They weren't servants. And since she didn't pay them wages, in cash, they weren't her employees. They were serfs, almost, like Russian peasants tied to the land, receiving just room and board for their labor. The simile made Didi uncomfortable.

She selected an apple, closed the refrigerator door, turned and said to Charlie: "We'll be leaving in about ten minutes."

"Where we going?" he asked.

"Out to Millerton, to vet a horse for Toby Broward."

"Damn!" Charlie exclaimed. "She already has six horses. Why does she need another one?"

Didi shot back crossly: "That's none of our business, Charlie. See you out front in ten minutes."

She had started out of the kitchen, toward the living room, when she heard Charlie say gently: "You know, Miss Quinn, we all die. Dick Obey got drunk, fell into a ditch, and died. That's all. He lived his life."

Didi froze. Why did he keep calling her Miss Quinn? Why not Didi? Or Miss Nightingale? Why use only her mother's maiden name? Sure, her father was long dead. But he had existed at one time. This was his farm, originally. And her mother had loved him. He was her father. It was her name.

"You have to accept God's will," she heard Mrs. Tunney say.

Didi turned on all of them in a fury, shouting: "It's not that he died. Don't you understand? It's the way he died. Dogs ripped his throat out! It's the horror of it that I can't stand!"

Then she shut up, as suddenly as she had exploded. There was an awkward silence. She turned on her heel and fled the room, still clutching her bread and apple.

* * *

As the crow flies, it is only twenty-five miles from Hillsbrook to Millerton, in the northeast corner of Dutchess County. But a jeep is not a crow, and the roads in that area are serpentine. So it was a forty-minute drive by jeep.

Ten minutes into the drive, Didi said to Charlie Gravis: "I had no right to shout at all of you in the kitchen, Charlie. I'm sorry."

Charlie made a motion with his hand that it was of no consequence. Didi started to put a tape in the deck but then thought better of it. After Dick Obey's death, any Patsy Cline music made her cry. She grasped the wheel tightly and tried to concentrate on the road.

Her outburst in the kitchen, she realized, had been fake. Oh, the passion and the hurt was not fake. But it was more about loss than horror. Dick Obey, she now realized, had played a very special role in her life. And he was the first true friend she had lost. Maybe he had been playing a role—as surrogate father. But so what? Everything about him was wonderful. He was a lean, handsome, work-hardened man who invariably called her "Vet." A man who was "country wise." Yes, that was it. He was the very model of what she had been looking for when she came back home—a social model of sorts. Almost a kind of guru. He had built and lost a fine dairy herd. He had loved and lost a wife. He had fathered and buried a son. He loved animals but would put one down in an instant if need be, without a trace of sentimentality. He treated her in a manner that could only be described as flirtatious respect, always. Sure, he drank. But three-quarters of the remaining dairy farmers in the county were probably alcoholics. It was the dairyman's disease. He didn't read and cared nothing for music, but he was the only man she had ever met who truly marveled at country sunsets.

The tears started to roll down Didi's cheeks as she drove. Yes, above all, she missed his country ways.

She remembered how, when they used to pass each other on the road, they would brake and each back the car up until they were side by side, with windows rolled down. And they would talk like that, right in the middle of the road, until either of them saw a car coming. His greeting was always the same: "Hey, Vet. Up early." Those car conversations were about nothing in particular but she had treasured them. Except when she saw he had been drinking, because then he seemed bitter and distant.

She blinked the tears away.

There was no conversation and no music until they reached Millerton. Toby Broward was waiting for them in the appointed place, standing in front of her ancient, light green Mercedes. She wore a raincoat over riding breeches.

"Pull the jeep up here. Mr. Thomas doesn't

like vehicles on his property," Toby explained. Didi pulled the jeep off the road as instructed.

Toby, Didi, and Charlie Gravis entered the Thomas property through a single unhinged gate. Mr. Thomas lived in a rusty trailer. Toby knocked on the door until the half-dressed man appeared. He said, sleepily: "Go on down to the stable. I'll be there soon."

Toby knew the way. As they walked she said to Didi: "He wants too much. But I think I can get him to come down. Anyway, I won't do a bloody thing until you tell me the horse is healthy."

They approached a row of well-built attached stalls that formed a semicircle around a grassy courtyard.

"Third stall on the left," Toby said, always looking directly at Didi and ignoring Charlie completely. It was obvious that Charlie and Toby disliked each other. Not a word had been spoken between them and Charlie muttered constantly to himself as he drudged behind the two young women.

Didi strode to the stall. The horse within stuck his head out to greet her.

"My God!" she murmured, stopping and staring at the animal's head.

"Jesus Christ Almighty!" she heard Charlie intone.

This horse was huge.

Toby Broward laughed and called out giddily,

like a happy schoolgirl: "Isn't he beautiful? I always wanted a draft horse. Ever since I saw those Clydesdales pulling the Budweiser wagon at the Dutchess County Fair."

Didi moved closer and peered into the stall. She had heard that there had been a revival of interest in draft horses: Suffolks, Percherons, Shires, Clydesdales, and other giant breeds. But this was the first one she had seen since she had returned to Dutchess County. Of course, their original function, in medieval times, was not on the farm but on the battlefield. They were bred for size and temperament and strength to carry knights in full armor.

And this one she was looking at was a beauty. It was a massive Old Style Belgium. Sometimes the breed was called Flemish. And he had the old style coloring—roan. The newer American representatives of the breed were usually chestnuts. And this one also had an adorable abundance of "feathers"—those ruffles around the bottom of each leg, like the decorations chefs put on drumsticks.

"Isn't he lovely?" Toby called out.

Didi didn't answer. She got to work. First she checked the stall for any metal strips which would have been installed if the horse "cribbed"—chewed compulsively on the wood. There were none.

She then took a large cube of sugar and held it up to the horse for a moment before enclosing it in her fist. The horse began to nuzzle her hand, searching for the goody. "In a minute, honey, in a minute," she cooed to the immense animal. As he nuzzled, she deftly inspected his teeth. By the worn cups on the upper intermediate incisors, she figured him to be about ten years old. She gave him the lump of sugar and said to Toby Broward: "He's close to ten."

"But Mr. Thomas said he was only seven," Toby protested.

Didi smiled at her. Mr. Thomas was trying to sell a horse. Toby blushed, then said: "I'll remember that during negotiations."

They both saw Mr. Thomas approaching them.

"Ready?" he asked.

"Take him out," Didi affirmed.

As Mr. Thomas led the horse out of the stall on a short halter, Didi watched the horse's eyes to make sure the pupils opened and closed in changing light conditions.

The man began to walk and trot the huge Belgium right in front of Didi. She noted the length of stride and evenness of gait. She looked for any hint of lameness or "padding"— where the feet go wide or interfere with each other.

Didi motioned to Mr. Thomas and he began to turn the Belgium in a slow circle so that she could identify any soreness or hock lameness.

She also listened carefully for whistling, heaves, asthma—any kind of "double-clutch" breathing.

She motioned again, just a quick sweep of her hand, and Mr. Thomas stopped the horse and held him still.

Crouching, Didi examined his front legs—foot, pastern, fetlock, cannon, knee. Then she went to the hind limbs—foot, pastern, fetlock, cannon, hock, gaskin, stifle, hip.

She stood up and walked slowly around the horse, studying him in his totality. Her hand brushed gently against his roan flanks. She felt a great affection for this giant.

Then she turned to Toby and said, loud enough so that Mr. Thomas could hear every word: "He's in good shape, Toby. Except for a capped hock on the left hind."

She showed Toby the firm swelling on the point of the hock, explaining that it wasn't serious . . . the horse wasn't lame . . . and it probably came from rubbing.

Then Mr. Thomas led the horse back into the stall. Toby Broward walked Didi and Charlie halfway back to the jeep. "Send me a bill," she said. She had become tense, almost abstract. She was about to negotiate for the gentle giant.

As the jeep drove off, Charlie Gravis said: "She needs that horse like I need wood ticks."

It was getting dark when the red jeep returned home. Didi and Charlie had made seven calls after the trip to Millerton to vet the giant horse, including a very difficult calving at John Theobold's dairy farm and a lacerated udder at Baille's farm in Pine Plains.

Once home, Didi went directly to the small animal clinic at the back of the house which also functioned as her office.

She sat down wearily at the cluttered desk and looked at the phone machine. The red light was blinking. She grabbed a pad and pencil, ready to make notes, and pushed the button.

There was only one message.

It was from a woman who identified herself as Emily Matthiessen. She said that Didi had been recommended highly to her. She said that it was an emergency . . . that her bird was quite ill. Could Didi return her call as soon as possible? Then she gave her number and hung up. The woman had not mentioned the time of her call.

Didi stared at the telephone number she had written on her pad as she listened to the message. The only strange thing about the call was the phone number. It had a Connecticut area code. Surely there were vets in Connecticut.

She dialed the number. A woman answered.

"Emily Matthiessen?"

"Yes?"

"This is Didi Nightingale."

"Oh! Thank you for calling back, Dr. Nightingale. My bird is very sick. She is lying at the bottom of her cage. She won't eat anything. Her eyes are glassy."

"Where do you live?" Didi asked.

"Kent, Connecticut."

"Well," Didi said, a bit confused, "I have a small animal clinic open two days a week. You can bring the bird in on Thursday. But surely, Miss Matthiessen, there is a vet close by to you in Kent."

"Yes, there are many. But you came recommended. I want you to look at her."

"Then bring her in on Thursday. Meanwhile, just keep her still and warm. You can put her in a sock."

The woman laughed over the phone, a bit hysterically. "No, I can't. It's a gray parrot."

Didi was silent. The woman begged: "Can't you come over now? It's only about forty minutes. Maybe less. I'm just over the state line."

"I'd be delighted to treat your gray parrot, Miss Matthiessen. Just bring her to the clinic on Thursday afternoon," Didi responded in her best professional voice—firm but compassionate.

The woman started to yell over the phone. Didi hung up. The woman was obviously too distraught to deal with. Maybe she would show up at the clinic . . . maybe she wouldn't.

Didi was tired, hungry, and dirty. She needed above all a shower and a meal, but she didn't move from that chair in front of the phone.

The sun had gone down. The small office was dark. She didn't put a light on. Damn! she thought. It would have to be a gray parrot! Of all the birds and beasts it would have to be a gray parrot. Her mother must be turning over in her grave, Didi sensed. Imagine not paying a house call on a gray parrot. Imagine not leaving immediately. Her mother had loved gray parrots above all creatures and that's why she tolerated those two mad birds—Hope and Charity—for all those years. Yes, her mother would have been appalled that her little daughter didn't just hop into her jeep and drive to Connecticut to treat the little darling. After all, according to her mother, gray parrots were very close to being human.

Didi laid her head down on her desk. She missed her mother even more than she missed Dick Obey. She wished her mother had lived to see her set up her own practice. She would have been so proud. But it was not to be.

Damn! Why did that woman have to have a sick gray parrot? No, her mother would not have approved of her conversation with Miss Matthiessen. Didi smiled suddenly. Her mother, in fact, had been more right than wrong about gray parrots. The new research showed that the gray parrot is probably the most intelligent and vocal of all birds. One gray parrot at a midwestern research center had already learned thirty concepts. The parrot could understand and communicate in English. Asked what color the popsicle is . . . the parrot studies the object and answers correctly—red.

Didi stood up. This kind of introspection had to stop. It was all nonsense. She started toward the kitchen, then stopped. She seemed to be hovering on a ledge . . . unsure whether to reach out or simply fall.

Then she reached for the phone and dialed.

A voice answered.

"Miss Matthiessen? This is Didi Nightingale again. . . . Yes . . . I'll be out to see your parrot tomorrow morning about seven-thirty. Please give me directions to your place."

Chapter Three

Didi arrived for her Connecticut appointment, alone in her red jeep, ten minutes early. She had decided against bringing Charlie Gravis, for no particular reason except that he above all had hated poor Hope and Charity and maybe he couldn't be neutral around any gray parrot. There was also the possibility that all gray parrots hated Charlie Gravis. Though this was not, she realized, a scientific point of view.

What a wonderful little place Emily Matthiessen had. It was one of those high, narrow, stone gate houses, overrun with ivy, attached to a stone arch which was attached to a stone pillar which had once anchored the gate of the estate. The gate and the estate, of course, were long gone. But the pillar and the arch and the stone house remained.

Didi hopped out of her jeep, suddenly joyous at such an architectural feast. She walked up to the studded wooden door and used the cast-iron knocker.

A tall, redheaded woman, about thirty, answered the door. She was wearing a dark green pantsuit. She was quite lovely. Her red hair was long and loose. She wore wire-rim glasses and Didi could see that she was reading a biography of T.H. White, a writer Didi had always loved.

"Dr. Nightingale?" she asked.

"Please call me Didi."

Once Didi was inside, the charm of the place increased. Everything was narrow and high. The entire house consisted of two rooms on the lower floor and a kind of planked attic that seemed to function as a storeroom, a circular staircase leading up to it.

There was little furniture. A small, high bed, almost an adult crib. A chest of drawers. A night table with a large lamp. Two ancient chairs. A rug. The other downstairs room had a sink and a stove and a small bathroom.

Didi felt relaxed, oddly at home.

"Would you like some coffee or tea?" Emily Matthiessen asked.

"No thanks. I stopped off on the way here. Show me the patient."

The tall redhead didn't move or speak. Didi waited . . . a bit confused . . . a bit apprehensive. Had the parrot died during the night?

Then Emily Matthiessen said: "There is no patient."

"What?"

"I have no gray parrot. It was a story I made up."

"But why?" Didi shot back, startled and angry and even more confused. She sat down on one of the chairs, staring angrily at the woman, but suddenly very weary.

"I had to speak to you alone."

"About what?"

"Dick Obey."

"How did you know Dick Obey?" Didi asked, even more startled.

"We were lovers."

Didi didn't know how to respond. Dick Obey had not mentioned any woman in his life. Ever. Other than his wife. And she was dead. Besides, this woman was young. Almost as young as Didi. Didi acknowledged a tiny thread of jealousy in her soul. Tiny but strong, gnawing. How could it be otherwise?

"Dick Obey paid for this house and he paid for the car parked out in front," Emily Matthiessen said.

"I find that incredible."

"I have proof."

"Who cares about your proof? Dick Obey was dead broke. He couldn't even pay the taxes on his place. Half the time he didn't have money to fill up his gas tank."

"You are very naive," Emily said.

Infuriated, Didi stood up and headed for the door.

"Please wait! Yes, I brought you here on a sham and I'm sorry. Dick told me about your mother's gray parrots, so I used that. But I have to tell you something very important. Dick Obey . . . your friend . . . my lover . . . was murdered."

"Why are you saying that?" Didi asked, so astonished that her words came out in a whisper. She backed away from the woman but also a little away from the door.

"He was murdered."

"Who would want to murder such a wonderful man?" Didi yelled, almost hysterical.

Emily Matthiessen didn't answer. She suddenly began to rummage around in the chest of drawers and finally, almost triumphantly, pulled out a garment.

She handed it to Didi, who refused to take it.

"It's for you," Emily said. "Dick bought it for you. You told him that you needed a garment like this for cold mornings, because it helped you stay warm but still have your hands free to conduct your examinations."

Didi took the beautiful serape almost reverentially in her arms and her anger and near hysteria dissolved. How did this strange woman know about her conversation with Dick—unless she was telling the truth about their intimacy. Yes, Didi had talked to Dick about a serape. But it never even occurred to her that Dick would buy her one. With what? He had no money.

"You see, except for the parrot, I have been honest with you," Emily Matthiessen said.

"All this is very confusing," Didi mumbled.

Emily Matthiessen went rummaging again . . . this time in the small kitchen. She came back with a plastic bag and carefully folded the serape into the bag and handed it back to Didi.

"I am sorry that I have upset you, Dr. Nightingale. But I had to get you here. I had to tell you what happened."

Didi's anger rose again—she was sick of all this cryptic nonsense. Who murdered him? Why? How? Was there any proof? Had this woman gone to the police? Was she truthful in some areas and delusional in others? Had Dick's death simply unhinged her? Why hadn't she been at the funeral?

Didi exploded: "What are you talking about? You didn't tell me anything that happened. You didn't tell me anything important."

"I told you that Dick Obey was murdered. Isn't that enough?"

And with that Emily Matthiessen flung the front door open. They had obviously both had enough of each other for the moment.

Didi sat in her jeep for about fifteen minutes without turning on the ignition. The serape was in her lap.

This strange woman had confused her

greatly. She didn't know what to think. If Emily Matthiessen had indeed been Dick Obey's lover—why had he concealed it? And where did he get the money to pay for her rent and transportation? And who on God's green earth would want to murder Dick Obey? Besides, the State Police in Delaware County had investigated. They had found that Dick died horribly but accidentally.

Suddenly Didi felt better. There was a good chance this woman, Emily Matthiessen, was a nut. Who else but a mentally deranged woman would have constructed such an elaborate ruse to get her to visit? The whole thing was off the wall.

She turned the ignition on and drove off. But she didn't rush home. She drove slowly, the serape on her knees evoking all kinds of memories. It would have been nice, she mused, if Dick Obey could have spent the last years of his life with someone he loved. It would be nice if the story was true—at least that part of it concerning their relationship.

Eventually she reached the environs of Hillsbrook again, but rather than go home she went to Inn Forty Four, the roadhouse where Dick Obey and his friends used to drink.

It was just past eleven o'clock. The bar was open, though lunch was not being served yet. Didi stood just inside the doorway and saw that

Roger Brice and Frank Draper were in their usual place at the end of the bar.

Roger Brice wore ancient coveralls and a baseball hat. His hands were powerful, misshapen, discolored and moldy—standard for a dairy farmer who spends most of the working year in one form of damp muck or another. He was a strongly built man in his midforties, with a full head of ungovernable sandy hair turning a bit gray.

Frank Draper dressed more carefully, with a corduroy jacket over his work clothes. He was younger than Brice and more aggressive personally. Since he was that rarest of all breeds in Dutchess County—a successful farmer—he acted the part, sometimes to the point of brashness. But his heart, as they say, was big, and in the right place.

A bottle of beer stood on the bar in front of each of the men. It was Frank Draper who saw Didi standing there, through the bar mirror. He turned on his stool and motioned her over.

She noticed that the last stool of the bar, the one against the wall, the one where Dick Obey always sat, was empty. She tried to avoid it and take the far stool, but Roger Brice guided her right into Dick's old seat.

"You look pale, girl," Roger Brice said.

Didi stared at herself in the mirror. Yes, she was pale. She looked, she realized, as if she had seen a ghost.

Frank Draper motioned to the bartender, who opened a bottle of beer and slid it in front of Didi. The idea of drinking beer at that hour of the day was incomprehensible to her.

"I heard something this morning," she said, speaking to both of them and to neither of them, speaking the words straight ahead.

"Well, that's good, honey," Frank Draper said, laughing, "because I heard nothing. I haven't heard anything in years, anything good, that is. And we all know if you're going to hear something good, it sure as hell isn't going to be told to you by a veterinarian."

Didi let the obligatory nonsense pass by. Then she said: "I heard that Dick Obey had been seeing a woman."

Roger Brice screwed up his face and ran his hand through his hair. "In Hillsbrook?" he asked.

"No. The woman lives in Kent."

"Connecticut?"

"Right."

The two men looked at each other. Brice said: "How wouldn't we have known about it, Didi? I saw Dick probably every day for the last fifteen years."

"Maybe he did see a woman once in a blue moon," Frank Draper suggested.

"No. This wasn't occasional. He paid her rent."

"What! You must be kidding. Dick couldn't

even pay for this," Frank Draper said, picking up the beer bottle, then letting it back down gently.

"Who told you this?" Brice asked.

"Someone."

"I wouldn't believe a word of it," Roger said.

Frank Draper said: "Dick told me that after his wife died . . . when was that? Nineteen eighty-five? Eighty-seven? . . . anyway, he told me that he went to Albany a few times and he was ashamed of himself."

"What was in Albany?" Didi asked.

"You know . . . Albany."

"No, I don't know."

"For women."

"You mean he went to a brothel in Albany."

"Yes."

"Why didn't he go to New York?" Didi asked.

"I don't know. He went to Albany."

The three sat in silence then, joined by memories of the fourth. From time to time they looked at each other in the mirror in front of them, as if they couldn't trust themselves to speak about Dick Obey because it was too painful, but they wanted each other to know Dick Obey was being thought about.

For a moment, for just a brief moment, Didi started to tell them what the woman had said— that Dick Obey had been murdered.

But then she stopped. She cut it off. The two men turned and waited. She said nothing more.

The atmosphere had become suddenly so oppressive that Roger Brice tried to make a feeble joke—about one of his best milking cows. It was a terrible joke and no one laughed, but it loosened up the situation enough so that Didi could leave easily. She drove home to pick up Charlie Gravis and start her rounds.

Chapter Four

It was the first truly springlike spring morning. The red jeep was headed toward Howard Danto's farm. Didi wanted to check the condition of the goats.

Halfway there, Charlie Gravis noted: "You're looking much better lately, Miss Quinn."

"Oh?" Didi responded angrily. "You mean I'm beginning to dress the way you and Mrs. Tunney want me to dress?"

Charlie realized his mistake. "No, no, Miss Quinn! I mean about how you kept grieving for Dick Obey. I mean grieving in a bad way. At least the first two weeks. Now you're better."

Then he lapsed into one of his arcane theories that the cycle of grief can't continue past thirty days and it had been thirty-two days since Dick Obey died, so she had to get better. Grieving, he said, was like pregnancy; when it's over, it's over. Didi let him babble on. What the hell did he know about pregnancy anyway? There's no fool like a wise old fool, she thought.

The goats turned out to be fine. Didi gave her new friend, the once-a-head-slamming doe, Laura, a treat, then she and Charlie headed back to the jeep, only to be greeted by Howard Danto, who stood in front of his house waving her over.

"I'll be back in a minute," she told Charlie.

As she approached he called out: "You must come in for a minute. I have something to give you." The last time she had seen him he was dressed bizarrely, in his idea of a farmer's work clothes. Now he had outdone himself, his idea of a farmer taking leisure. He wore a silk scarf and a patched corduroy jacket and beautiful doeskin pants with shined half boots. One didn't know whether to laugh or cry.

It was worse when she got inside. The old house was a lovely, sprawling thing, but Danto had obviously hired a decorator with a New Mexico fetish. It was impressive but seemed very out of place in Upstate New York. The place was a minimalist Mexican hacienda.

"Your goats are fine," she said.

He nodded happily. "Can you call me Howard and can I call you Didi?" he asked.

"Of course."

Danto sat down at a beautiful, long polished table and wrote a check. He ripped it out of the book with a flourish and handed it to Didi.

"You don't have to pay me now. I send out bills on the first of the month."

"Well, you're here," he said, "so take it."

She hesitated. "Besides," he said, "you didn't send me a bill this month. I never received one." Didi didn't want to start explaining that she had neglected all of her office work because of Dick Obey's death, so she took the check.

It was for five hundred dollars!

"Wait a minute," she said. "Your bill won't even be a third of this."

"Then credit my account for the rest," he said.

Didi folded the check and put it into her jacket pocket. "Thank you," she said.

"I have a new espresso machine," he said happily. "Can I interest you in a cup?"

"Charlie is waiting for me in the jeep. We have other stops to make. Perhaps next time."

His face collapsed suddenly, as if her simple refusal was just too much for him to bear.

"Of course, of course, I understand," he finally spluttered, "but before you go I must tell you something."

Didi waited patiently. The large man seemed to struggle for words, nervously playing with his scarf.

"I am afraid," he said, "that I have developed a passion for you."

Didi didn't know what to say. It was a standing joke in veterinary school that male vets would have to fight off amorous female riders of the horses they treated. But no one ever said anything about women vets and gentlemen goat herders.

Then she replied playfully: "I think, Howard, you are making a pass at me."

"I'm afraid I am," he confessed in a mournful voice as if he were truly ashamed of himself.

He looked so terribly sad that Didi felt she had to do something. All she could remember was that old bromide her mother used to utter. She took out her sunglasses and put them on; then she modified the bromide: "Howard, farmers seldom make passes at vets who wear glasses." It went over like a lead balloon. She took the glasses off quickly and said: "Well, I will bear that in mind . . . your passion, that is. At least you are an honest man, Howard."

She waved at him . . . let herself out the front door . . . and walked quickly to the waiting jeep.

Didi and Charlie finished their rounds by early afternoon and headed home. Today was small animal clinic hours and Didi liked to be there with time to spare.

But a patient was already waiting for her. None other than Bucket, the large Labrador/bloodhound mixed breed, accompanied by his master, John Theobold, one of the men who served on the rabies committee with her.

Bucket was wearing a muzzle and the indignity of it elicited very sad moans from him. He was a lovable, difficult, floppy hound who roamed John Theobold's dairy farm. If there was trouble to get into, Bucket would find it. The last time Bucket had been her patient, he had somehow gotten a marrow bone over his lower jaw and Didi had to saw it off with a fine wire.

Didi knelt beside the unhappy hound. "Hello, Bucket! What kind of trouble have you gotten into this time?" He moaned some more. She scratched him behind the ear. Who on earth would want to cross a Lab with a bloodhound?

"He's the stupidest dog in existence," said the soft-spoken John Theobold, who was sometimes called Abe by his neighbors in Hillsbrook because of his uncanny resemblance to Lincoln.

"Why the muzzle?"

"He's been chewing his damn leg off. I tried one of those collars but he got it off. I bandaged it, but he ripped the bandage. I put mustard on it, but he licked the mustard off like it was gravy and kept at it."

"Help me up with him," Didi said.

Together they lifted the unhappy beast onto the examining table. It was, indeed, an ugly hot spot, down low on the inside of the left hind leg. He had chewed himself almost to the bone.

Didi got some gauze and began to clean the wound with an antiseptic wash. These hot spots were always a problem with some dogs. And one could never be sure as to the cause. Sometimes it was a skin allergy. Sometimes a bacterial infection. Sometimes just a foreign body like a small burr. Whatever the cause, the afflicted dog then begins to lick or chew to alleviate the symptom . . . and, in many cases, that licking or chewing becomes a compulsive behavior. When it becomes compulsive, it can be serious.

Bucket's wound was now so deep it had to be considered serious.

"I have a very good collar for him. Do you want to try that, John?" She went to a closet and pulled out one of those corset contraptions that went all around the neck so that the dog wearing it looked like Queen Elizabeth.

"Believe me, Didi, they don't work. He gets them off by rubbing against wire fences. Sooner or later he gets them off."

"Yes," Didi said, staring at Bucket, "I believe you."

She put the collar back into the closet and returned with a strong disinfectant. She doused the wound.

"Take off the muzzle, John."

Theobold slipped the muzzle off. Bucket seemed to grin, then immediately flopped down on the table and began to chew at the wound, oblivious to the powerful disinfectant that had been applied.

Frustrated, Didi tried to push his head away. Bucket growled and snapped at her.

Theobold slapped him on the nose and put the muzzle back on.

Bucket started to moan again. Didi wondered if this was the time to test the power of Charlie Gravis's legendary potion, called, ridiculously, Dandelion Juice.

Actually, she wouldn't give a penny for any of old Charlie's supposed herbal cures. But a dozen people had told her that this potion really worked for hot spots. Charlie brewed it outside from rotten apples and dried leaves, along with vinegar and god knows what else. She hated to give Charlie an inch on this matter, because he would start bothering her to dispense other remedies, something she had already squelched successfully.

But why not? What did Bucket have to lose?

"I'll be right back, John," she said, and walked into the kitchen where Charlie was drinking a cup of coffee.

"Charlie! John Theobold brought Bucket in. He has a bad hot spot. I wonder if you have any of your remedy handy."

Charlie Gravis put the cup down slowly, and began to grin; it was one of those grins that said . . . "well, I knew that sooner or later you were going to see the light." But then, when Charlie realized that Didi was getting angry, he wiped the grin off his face and said, deadpan: "Get the patient ready."

Didi turned on her heel and walked back into

the clinic. God, she thought, sometimes that old man is insufferable.

Charlie came into the clinic five minutes later, acting very much the veterinarian-in-residence.

He was carrying an old milk bottle filled with the ugliest-looking fluid imaginable, green and yellow, capped by a piece of cloth fastened with thick rubber bands.

"Put the dog on the floor," he said. Once Bucket was safely down, Charlie asked Didi: "May I have a gauze pad, please?"

Didi gritted her teeth, got a pad, stripped the paper off, and handed it to him.

Playing up the drama, Charlie poured some of the brew onto the pad and applied it vigorously to the hot spot.

Then he said: "Okay. Let Bucket at it."

Theobold slipped the muzzle off again. Bucket flopped down and went for the hot spot.

He took one lick, then pulled his head away and stood up. He looked in shock. He started to spit. He started to circle. He had this wild look in his eyes. He seemed totally confused.

Then he plopped down again and went for the hot spot. Again, he took only one lick and spat.

Then he just sat there. He didn't go for the spot again.

"Damn!" John Theobold exclaimed. "It worked."

Charlie Gravis gave him an arch look, as if this were the only possible outcome.

"Just put a little on the wound each morning and each night," Charlie instructed, "until it clears up." Charlie walked to the counter to fill a small flask for Theobold.

"It must taste terrible," the dairy farmer mused.

"Beyond your wildest dreams," Charlie said triumphantly. "But remember, it takes a couple of months' brewing time before it gets to tasting that terrible."

Didi shook her head but said nothing. So much for veterinary science.

After John and Bucket left and Charlie went happily on his way, Didi stayed in the clinic office until 4:30 P.M. There were no more patients. She was tired and hungry. She walked into the kitchen to make herself a sandwich.

Mrs. Tunney was at the counter pounding some meat. Abigail was seated at the long table cutting up potatoes.

Didi smiled at Abigail, who nodded in return. The young woman was a cipher, and very shy to boot. Didi liked her very much but found herself unable to converse with her . . . and she had no idea whatsoever what kind of life Abigail had outside the house—if indeed she had any. All Didi knew about her was that Mrs. Tunney's cousin's daughter had married a man called Luke; that Abigail was the child of that union;

that her father had died and her mother had remarried and moved to Maine; and that Abigail herself had once attended some kind of music school in Rochester but had to leave suddenly because of unspecified problems. And none of that information could really be verified.

Didi began to prepare her cheddar cheese sandwich with tomato. She sliced the ingredients very thin and covered both pieces of bread liberally with mustard.

Mrs. Tunney said: "Supper will be ready in about an hour."

"I'm tired, Mrs. Tunney, so I think I'll pass. But thank you for asking."

Mrs. Tunney clucked disapprovingly, even though Didi never ate any meals with them.

Carrying the sandwich and a small bottle of ginger ale, Didi went to her wing of the house and climbed the stairs to her bedroom.

It was an enormous room, covering virtually the entire north end of the house. One could look out of the many windows—nine in all—and see a wide swatch of property, from the road to the pine forest.

This had been her mother's bedroom and Didi hadn't changed a single thing after she died, although she didn't like the massive furniture scattered throughout, which her mother had picked up over the years at country auctions. Nothing in the room matched. Nothing in the room fit. Except for the two stuffed chairs by the windows. These Didi loved. She had loved them as a child and she loved them now.

She ate the sandwich in one of those chairs, leafing through the current issue of *Audubon*. The feature article was about certain vanishing Indian tribes of the Amazon rain forest. She found the pictures beautiful but she was too tired to concentrate. Finally, she turned the floor lamp out and just sat there, relaxed, musing over the day's events.

A terrible noise battered her head. She leaped up and looked around wildly.

Then she realized that she had been asleep, that she had fallen asleep in the easy chair. The room was dark. The house was dark. The luminous clock dial read 10:20. She realized that she had been asleep for almost five hours.

The noise came again, like an explosion. She turned toward the window. A sheet of rain smashed into the panes, shaking them furiously. It was thunder that she was hearing. Then the rain and thunder ceased as quickly as they had come, and the weird, frightening pyrotechnics of an electrical storm illuminated the entire property. Didi sat back down, cold, frightened. She closed her eyes. She reached back and pulled the garment hanging on the back of the chair over her.

The storm passed. She opened her eyes and

turned on the floor lamp. The crust from her sandwich had fallen on the floor. She scooped it up.

Her eyes caught something strange in the night. Through the window, on the far side of the road, she could see a tremendous surge of light. It was quite beautiful. But the lightning had passed. She was confused. It became brighter and brighter and began to pulse.

Suddenly her legs felt weak. She realized what she was seeing. A fire! And it was Dick Obey's place.

She ran down the stairs and out of the house. Trent Tucker and Abigail were already down there, staring at the fire.

Didi climbed into the jeep and motioned for them to join her. They didn't hesitate. It is the iron law of country living that neighbors go to fires to help out in any way they can.

The first volunteer fire companies arrived at the scene the same time as Didi. There was little, however, that anyone could do. The main house, the barn, and the three sheds were shrouded in flames—white and blue and hot.

The heat became so intense that they had to move back onto the road to escape it. More and more engines came. And more neighbors.

Then the buildings began to implode, just crumbling into themselves like burst paper bags. Torrents of sparks shot skyward.

Didi felt a sadness so profound she could

scarcely sit straight over the wheel. She wanted to lie down on the ground and weep. Dick Obey had loved his farm so much. Even after the dairy operation had gone under, he used to tell her about his dreams of starting up again. This time, he said, he was going to get a herd of those new cross-bred cows; bred to beef cattle so that they could turn pasture into milk. That way, even with lower milk production per cow, the farmer makes money because he doesn't have those huge feed bills. The cows feed themselves on pasture.

Yes, he had talked a lot about that. She grew colder and pulled the garment tightly around her. Then she realized that she was wearing the serape that strange woman had given her . . . the serape that Emily Matthiessen said Dick Obey had purchased for Didi as a gift.

Didi started to cry. she couldn't help herself. Abigail and Trent Tucker turned away in embarrassment.

Didi started the jeep and drove back to the house. She parked but didn't get out. Trent and Abigail went into the house. Trent called back once: "Those electrical storms are bad news. It could have been any property. It could have been this house."

Didi turned in her seat and stared back at the fire. It had diminished greatly because of the collapse of the buildings. For the first time she could see long lines of water arcing out of the fire hoses. Smoke still filled the air, probably for miles around.

The sadness and the tears left her. She sat straight and grasped the wheel tightly.

A terrible clarity began to emerge. For the first time she saw a sequence . . . a progression. It was quite simple. First Dick Obey was destroyed. And then his farm was destroyed.

She realized she did not believe the fire was started by the electrical storm.

And, for the first time, she believed everything that strange woman in Connecticut had told her . . . especially that Dick Obey was murdered.

Chapter Five

The Hillsbrook Police Department was temporarily quartered in a large construction-type trailer. One approached it by turning into an alley just west of the bookstore on the main street, and walking about fifty yards in.

The department had grown to eight, double the size of the force when Didi had left Hillsbrook to go to college. The reason for the growth was not simply the population rise in the Hillsbrook area but the new *kinds* of populations. Many religious organizations and foundations had purchased estates and farms . . . and breaking into them had become a sort of hobby among the less ethical denizens of the area. In addition, at least two long-term drug rehab facilities had moved to the area and many of their inhabitants seemed to be perpetually wandering the country roads, creating anxiety among the long-time residents, even though these wanderers were seldom disruptive.

Didi entered a bit nervously. The trailer was

jammed with all kinds of radio and electronic equipment. Along one wall was a banner: SUP-PORT UNITED WAY.

Two men were talking in the trailer's narrow aisle, which led to the small kitchen and toilet. One was a uniformed Hillsbrook officer. The other was a burly man with longish hair, dressed in jeans and a red shirt.

Didi was about to approach them when the man in the red shirt turned, saw her, and let out a shout: "Damn! It's Didi Nightingale!" He walked toward her, grinning, his hand outstretched.

She shook his hand but she didn't know who he was or how he knew her.

"Do you mean you don't remember me?" he asked, humorously but accusingly. "You mean you don't remember Allie Voegler? I was one year ahead of you in high school."

The name did ring a bell. She stared at the young man. Gradually a memory formed, grew, opened up. Then she remembered clearly. He had been one of the wild kids—a motorcyclist. She had avoided him and his friends like the plague.

"Well," she said, smiling, "at least you didn't turn out to be a Hell's Angel."

"No. But I didn't turn out to be a hot-shot veterinarian like yourself, either."

"All I do," she replied, "is take care of dairy cows."

The uniformed police officer who had been talking to Voegler walked out of the trailer with a "catch you later."

"Well, what can I do for you?" he asked her expansively.

"I want to report a murder," she said. The moment the words popped out she realized they sounded stupid, weird—but there was no other way to phrase it.

He gave her one of those quick "am I dealing with a nut?" looks, then recovered and asked, professionally: "Whose murder?"

"Dick Obey," she replied.

He shot back: "No! You can't report Dick Obey's murder. I have the Delaware County coroner's report. Dick Obey fell drunk into a ditch and was killed by a pack of dogs."

"He was murdered," Didi corrected adamantly.

"Do you have any proof of this?" Allie Voegler asked. His voice was becoming aggressive. She was beginning to irritate him.

"His mistress told me he was murdered." She wondered why she had used that old-fashioned word.

"Does *she* have anything to support such a charge?"

"I don't think so. In fact, I didn't believe her at first."

"But now you do?"

"Yes."

"Why?"

"Because of the fire."

"It was an electrical storm."

"No," Didi said. "It was arson."

"You have anything to substantiate *that*?"

"It was arson," she repeated.

"Sure," he said sarcastically, then indicated with his hands that this interview was over. He smiled. "I'll take what you told me under advisement."

But Didi wasn't through.

"I want to see the crime-scene photos from Delaware County."

"Oh, do you?"

"Do you have them?"

He exploded. "Of course not. Why the hell would I need to look at them? I told you what was in the coroner's report. And it confirmed the state trooper report. Besides, there are no *crime*-scene photos. It was an accident."

"Well, I'd like to see them."

"Look, why don't you stick with cows and I'll take care of the crime. Okay?"

"Believe me. I can see things you can't," she said gently.

"Yeah, I suppose you can read a lot of things in a field of cowshit."

She ignored the provocation. "I'm trained in something that is very close to forensic medicine. I investigate 'crimes' against animals all the time. The perpetrators may be bacteria or viruses or allergies or cruel masters—but the investigative method is the same."

"I don't want to hear that nonsense," he replied. "Look, you're a taxpayer. You're a pillar of the community and a vet to boot. Sure, you are. So I'll give you a damn letter. You can get all the crime-scene photos you want. If that's the way you get your kicks, that's fine with me. I guess that's what you learned in Philadelphia. That's where you went to vet school, isn't it?"

He strode to the small typewriter on a table at the other side of the trailer. He slammed a piece of paper into the carriage. Didi noted the incongruity of the machine . . . an old-fashioned manual standing amid new hi-tech computer terminals and telecommunication machines. Voegler announced: "I'm going to write you a personal letter to the Delaware County Coroner's Office. It's police courtesy. They'll give you what you want, as a favor to the Hillsbrook Police Department. But do me a favor. Don't bother me anymore. I realize now why we never liked each other in high school."

Didi didn't reply. He finished the letter with a flourish, ripped it out of the machine, pressed some kind of rubber stamp to it, signed it, made a copy on a portable copying machine, folded it, and handed it to her.

She said: "Thank you." Allie Voegler turned his back and began to busy himself with something. It was obvious that he considered the meeting over.

But Didi didn't leave. "You know," she said in a kindly voice, "I didn't dislike you in high school. I was just frightened of you and your friends."

He looked at her, his eyes squinting. "Right. You were frightened of the motorcycle exhausts. But I guess little girls like you who live in big houses are always frightened of boys who ride cycles."

"Do you think my family was rich?" she asked incredulously.

"I didn't say you were rich. I said you lived in a big house."

"But you implied it."

"If the shoe fits, wear it."

There was an awkward silence. Then he said: "You know, I liked Dick Obey very much . . . and if there was any chance that the coroner's report was inaccurate . . . if there was one shred of evidence that someone murdered him . . . I would be on it. You can bet your last dollar on that."

Didi started to walk out.

"Wait!" Allie Voegler's command was very abrupt. He approached her. It was obvious he was very angry now. "You want to know why I'm so irritated? You really want to know? I'll tell you. Because you're damn arrogant. You just walk in here like you own the whole goddamn town and you announce to me that Dick Obey was murdered. You don't ask. You don't speculate. You just damn announce it. Like I'm supposed to hang on your every word like the gospel."

The force of his anger astonished Didi. Here was a grown man who still seemed obsessed with adolescent injuries, real and imagined. High school was a long time ago. What kind of fool was this man? But then she realized he was using those memories to protect himself now. After all, she was questioning his professionalism and his skill as a police officer. This conversation, she realized, had gotten out of hand and was going nowhere.

"I'm sorry my tone of voice was aggressive. I didn't mean it to be."

"You were like that in high school, Didi Nightingale. You and your friends always acted like you knew it all. But you didn't know it all . . . did you? You probably couldn't make it in the big city so you ended up right back here, like all of us who never left."

"I came back because I want to practice veterinary medicine here. Because it is where my family lived and worked and died. If you can't understand that, what's the point of continuing this conversation?"

"We're not having a conversation."

"Correct, Officer Voegler." She walked out.

Chapter Six

It had been one of those inexplicable early morning accidents. A Ford Bronco, driven by a woman with three kids in the back, had hit a deer on Route 44.

The deer had died instantly but flipped up onto the hood. Two of the hoofs had gone through the front windshield and severely lacerated the driver, who then lost control of the vehicle, spun across the divider, forced two cars off the road, then came to rest on the shoulder.

Many injuries but no deaths—except for the deer.

Allie Voegler had arrived on the scene too late to really be of any help, so he stayed in the car and watched uniformed Hillsbrook police, New York State Troopers, and EMS personnel clean up the mess.

His mind was elsewhere, anyway. It had been three days since Didi Nightingale had come to the trailer, and he was still obsessed with the meeting. Her claims had irritated him. Her speech had irritated him. Her patronizing arrogance had infuriated him. Above all, he was embarrassed as hell that he had lost his cool and shouted at her.

Allie drummed the wheel of his car with his fingers. He stewed in the memory. He knew that his anger at her had roots in the past. In high school he had had an enormous crush on her and she had ignored him. He interpreted the rejection as snobbery . . . she looked down on him. He was village trash. Dairy farmers always thought themselves god's own chosen people. Even after they didn't have a single cow left to milk.

He checked the time. He still had an hour before he was officially on duty. He kept drumming his fingers. The Obey place was only five minutes away. Why not check it out? Why not show Didi Nightingale what a fool she was.

Allie Voegler started the engine and drove slowly to Dick Obey's property. He parked the car on the shoulder, removed a crowbar from the trunk, and walked onto the property.

What a dismal scene it was! There were deep furrows in the earth, crisscrossing every which way, made by the fire fighting equipment. The house and the barn and the sheds were rubble.

He hesitated. What the hell was he doing there? Why had he let Didi Nightingale get to him? And why would anyone burn down a dead man's buildings? Maybe Dick Obey did owe someone a lot of money. But the angry creditor would seek vengeance while Dick Obey was alive. Not after he was dead. It made no sense at all. And the bank owned the property now. Arson for insurance fraud made no sense either. The buildings were worth nothing and the bank didn't care whether they were standing or not. It was the land that was worth money.

Well, he was already on the premises. He might as well conduct some kind of investigation, even if he wasn't a fire marshal.

Allie Voegler approached what was left of the house first. It was a grim pile of rubble: bent pipes jutting every which way; charred wood; and kitchen appliances melted out of shape. He dug at the corners with his crowbar, not knowing what he was looking for. Allie quickly realized how futile his task was. It would require ten men and ten days to really search through the debris for any clues to arson.

He walked toward the remains of the three sheds. All that was left of each was collapsed kindling wood.

He wondered where the lightning had struck first. Wherever, it must have ignited quickly and then thrown off sparks that ignited the other buildings. Or it could have been ground lightning, the most dangerous aspect of electrical storms. All the buildings could have ignited at once.

By the side of the second shed he spotted

tiny tufts of feathers along the ground. There hadn't been any chickens in those sheds for years. Perhaps pigeons or doves or owls had made the sheds their home. Whatever birds they were, they obviously hadn't gotten out in time. Or they had been killed in the initial lightning strike.

He walked on . . . to the collapsed charred barn. At least here he could make out a recognizable structure because the tile milking stalls and the aluminum runners and the stainless steel piping were still visible—twisted but visible.

The morning had turned beautiful. Strong sun and soft breeze. Allie stared at the sky for a moment and his anger resurfaced. "What the hell am I doing here?" he muttered out loud, bringing the crowbar down hard on some charred beams. The wood splintered like glass.

He started toward the car.

Suddenly, his eye caught a flash of color . . . green . . . in the rubble toward the front of the barn. He blinked. Was it the sun playing tricks?

He moved closer. No, it surely was something odd. He walked to the spot and crouched down.

Not green—turquoise. A piece of turquoise beading was wedged between charred wood. He moved the wood away with his crowbar.

It was turquoise beading like the Navajo make and it was part of what once was a Western-style boot. He pulled it out. The top and the tongue had been burned away. All the remaining leather was discolored. But the design, the beading, which had obviously run along both sides of the boot, was intact.

Odd, very odd. Dick Obey didn't wear that kind of shoe. And working firemen don't wear Western-style boots.

A lot of people in Dutchess County, New York, listen to country and western music. But not many wear Western hand-tooled boots. They're not for work or even for walking in mud.

Whoever owned these boots, Allie knew, didn't get them in Hillsbrook. There was only one shoe store in the village and it was decidedly conservative.

No, it would have to have been purchased at Agway. The big farm implement and grain dealer outside of Hillsbrook now carried everything in consumer goods. And they opened early. He walked quickly to his car, placed the remains of the boot gingerly on the seat beside him, and drove off.

Fifteen minutes later he was holding the burnt remains up to a perplexed Arthur Satchel, one of the two owners of the Agway franchise just outside Hillsbrook.

"It may have been one of ours," Arthur finally said.

"Recently?" Allie pressed.

"No, no. Maybe five years ago. The manufacturer was in Wyoming, if I remember. They made fancy Western boots and we took just five pair to see how they would sell. Yes. I remember the turquoise beading. We sold them quick enough but couldn't get any more because the company went out of business."

"Do you remember who bought them?"

"No. It was a long while back."

"The receipts?"

"No. We save them for one calendar year."

"What about your partner? Maybe he remembers."

The man shrugged and called his partner over. His name was Mack Bellio. Allie showed him the boot.

"Do you remember this?" Arthur Satchel asked his partner.

"Sure. But they looked a lot prettier then."

"I need to know who bought them."

"I only remember one customer. Only one. That crazy Brice kid."

Bingo. "Trevor Brice?" Allie Voegler pressed, naming Roger Brice's oldest son; a young man who had spent most of the years between ages fifteen and twenty in various penal institutions because he had a passion and a talent for stealing cars.

Allie Voegler himself had arrested young Brice at least three times since he had been on the force. Young Brice, of late, seemed to have turned over a new leaf. He no longer stole cars.

He seemed to spend most of his time now searching for booze and sex, once in a great while showing up at his long-suffering father's barn.

"Who else?" replied the store owner, signifying that turquoise-beaded Western-style boots were right up Trevor Brice's alley. At least, five years ago they were.

Allie Voegler left Agway quickly, with the remains of the boot now safely wrapped in a large sheet of gift wrap.

He drove to the Brice farm. The cows were already out in the pasture. Roger Brice was measuring out dietary supplements using an archaic funnel in front of his main barn. He greeted Allie nervously.

"Is there any trouble?" he asked.

"No trouble at all," Allie assured him. "I just want to talk to Trev."

"Well, he's upstairs, still sleeping. Why don't you just go right in and wake him up and tell him his daddy could use a little help."

"The wife inside?" Allie asked, nervous about going to the house unaccompanied.

"She's away for a few days, visiting," Brice answered. Allie nodded and walked into the farmhouse and padded slowly and carefully up the stairs.

Only one bedroom door was shut. All the other rooms were empty. He knocked twice and walked in.

Trevor Brice was not sleeping. He was lying on the bed in pajama bottoms, smoking a cigarette.

The room was an unholy mess. Trevor looked even worse; a monumental hangover. The cheekbones of his thin face were puffed up. His thick brown hair looked as if it had been parted by a tornado.

"Did you bring coffee, Officer Voegler?" Trevor Brice quipped.

"No. I brought you back your boot," Allie replied, opening the wrapping paper and letting the mutilated leather fall onto the bed beside the young man.

Trevor Brice didn't blink an eye. He looked at the object casually and arched his eyebrows just a bit, as if Allie Voegler should be ashamed of himself for throwing such an atrocity on his pristine bed.

"What is it?" he finally asked.

"What I said it was— a boot. Part of a boot."

"I don't wear boots. They hurt my toes."

"Are you sure that wasn't your boot, Trevor? Look at the beading."

Trevor Brice exhaled. He didn't look at the object. He smiled at Allie. "I told you—it's not my boot."

Allie sat down on the edge of the bed. He knew he had the kid. If Trevor had admitted the boot was his, the kid might have been hard to break. But he lied. And Allie knew he was going to pin Trevor Brice to the wall before he walked out of that bedroom. He grinned. He relished the idea that very soon he would be able to point out to Miss Didi Nightingale just how ridiculous she was.

"Are you sure it isn't your boot?" Allie asked softly, beginning the interrogation.

Chapter Seven

It was an overcast morning. In the backyard of the house, Didi was again in the lotus position. She was deep into the last part of her breathing exercises. First, she had just breathed in and out deeply, trying to maintain a steady rate of inhalation and exhalation. Then she had gently alternated pressing one nostril closed and breathing in and out through the other nostril. Now she was in the most difficult part of the breathing exercises—the one that was supposed to end the cloudiness and confusion of mental images and thought—the retention of both inhalation and exhalation.

She still couldn't do it properly, but she kept on trying.

It was just as she achieved that momentary balance between discomfort and repose that she saw the shadow of a man.

For some reason it frightened her, and she got to her feet so quickly that her leg cramped.

As she bent over and began to massage the

cramp furiously, she started to snap at Trent Tucker . . . who was the only one it could be and who should know better. She did not ask much from her "retainers"—the one thing she *did* ask was that they leave her alone during her morning yoga.

But it was not Trent.

It was a grinning Allie Voegler, standing there like a puffed-up bear, all full of himself.

"What the hell are you doing?" he asked.

"Breathing. Yoga."

"Well," he said, "different strokes for different folks."

Didi proceeded to knead out the cramp.

"I just came by to tell you something. To let you know that you were absolutely right about the fire at Dick Obey's place. It wasn't from the electrical storm. It wasn't lightning that started the fire."

He paused for a minute, then his voice became positively gleeful.

"But everything else you told me, Miss Nightingale, was nonsense. Total nonsense! It wasn't arson. Trevor Brice had a load on and was driving home. The storm came up. He took refuge in Dick Obey's barn. The rain was so ferocious that he had to take his boots off because they had become soaked. He waited in the barn until the storm was over. He finished a bottle. He lit a cigarette. He fell asleep. When he awoke the whole place was on fire. He ran out so fast he left his boots."

His manner disgusted Didi. He looked like a kid who had just won a bet about a baseball player's batting average and was now crowing and waiting to collect his bubble gum.

"Interesting," Didi said.

"Is that all you can say?" he half shouted.

"Do you have five minutes to spare, Mr. Voegler?"

"Officer Voegler. Or Allie. Don't call me Mister."

"Whatever you wish. But do you have five minutes?"

"For what?"

"I want to show you something."

"Sure," he said expansively. "I like women with vivid imaginations."

Didi walked into the house and through the kitchen, followed by Allie Voegler. He was greeted warmly by Mrs. Tunney but the other breakfasters just stared at him in bewilderment. One of the dogs grabbed Allie's cuff and started to worry it playfully.

Trent Tucker pulled the dog off, saying: "I guess he don't like the Hillsbrook Police."

Allie Voegler didn't reply. He followed Didi into her small animal clinic. She closed the door and switched the lights on.

"Take a look," she said, pointing at the illuminated board on which she usually attached and studied X-rays.

Affixed to the board were nine full-color, high-definition crime-scene photos. They were grisly. They were closeups of Dick Obey's face and neck and arms.

"So you really went and got them," Allie said, staring at the photos.

"I really did."

"So what?" he asked flippantly.

Didi picked up a pencil and tapped the eraser part on the first four photos—the ones that, in tandem, gave a complete 360-degree view of Dick Obey's mutilated neck.

"What do you make of the wounds?" she asked.

"Ugly. But stray dog packs sometimes go crazy."

"Did you ever see those dead deer that were run down by stray dogs?" she asked.

"Of course," he replied angrily. "Everyone who grew up around here has seen them."

She waited for him to say more. But all he said was: "What the hell are you getting at?"

"I'll tell you. You see how the entire circumference of the neck was savaged by the dogs? Well, feral dogs do not feed that way. They revert to their primitive instincts. First the dogs rip out the jugular of the dying prey. They rip out the front of the neck. Then they immediately proceed to the stomach . . . unless the rest of the body is not accessible to them."

She could see that her words were beginning to unnerve him. He moved closer to the photos.

Didi continued. "Here is what obviously happened, Officer Voegler. Dick Obey was either strangled or garroted. Then blood was poured over his neck, all around his neck. Maybe Obey's blood. Maybe chicken blood. That way, the dogs would feed all around the neck, obliterating the rope or wire marks. Then the dogs were driven away . . . which is why no part of his body was mutilated."

She waited for a response. But all Allie Voegler did was sit down.

Didi touched another photo with her pencil. "And look at these strange marks on his left wrist. Bites maybe. But not from dogs. I can't really tell what kind of animal did it. And I don't know what they signify."

She tapped the pencil several times in her palm. "Here's what we do know. The bites of the dog pack were not made when he was alive and drunk. He was executed. The dogs were lured to mutilate the entire neck."

She waited. She realized now that Allie Voegler had been stunned by her analysis.

"Well? What do you think of my veterinary skills?" she asked, a bit aggressive.

He looked at her, wide-eyed and respectful. "I believe you," he said simply.

"Then you'll come with me to interview that woman in Connecticut?" she asked.

"I'm ready," he replied.

Chapter Eight

They drove to Kent, Connecticut, early that afternoon, in Allie Voegler's car. Didi noticed that
he was distinctly nervous; he kept his eyes
straight ahead and constantly turned the radio
on and off.

About ten minutes into the ride, the reason
for his nervousness became clear—he was having second thoughts.

"What you told me about those photos," he
said, "seemed right. It seemed very right. But
that was this morning. Now, I don't know.
There could be other explanations. It doesn't
prove anything."

"You mean you don't think Dick Obey was
murdered?"

"I mean I don't know. I'm going with you just
to see if we should open an investigation. You
should have questioned the woman further,
anyway, the first time you talked to her. You
should have gotten something concrete . . .
something we could hang our hat on."

"I don't wear hats," Didi replied, a bit mockingly. She wasn't going to let Allie Voegler irritate her. Since she had begun to study the photos, she had been on a strange kind of high. She had easily made the transition from evaluating animal traumas to evaluating a specific human's morbidity. That the photos were of her friend just made it more intense. She had always had a flair for diagnosis; even her professors in Philadelphia had remarked on that. But that flair was always attributed by her and others to the strange empathy she had with animals . . . a gift she had even as a child. She had never been known as a particularly warm person toward other humans. But with those crime-scene photos—everything seemed to coalesce. Everything. She knew what she was looking at with a fierce confidence . . . and with intimacy.

"How do you like it back here?" Allie Voegler asked, changing the subject.

"I like it," she said.

"I see you still have that crew at your house. Were they left to you in your mother's will?"

She smiled. "Something like that."

They made the rest of the trip in silence. As they approached the Connecticut state line Didi leaned forward and began to direct him. There were several turns and detours that had to be made, but she remembered every one of them.

Finally they pulled up in front of the lovely little stone gate house.

The moment she stepped out of the car, Didi felt that something was wrong. There was litter on the approach to the house and the small high windows were shut tight.

With Allie Voegler right behind her, she knocked loudly on the door. No answer. She stepped back and yelled a few "hellos." No answer.

She turned the knob. The door swung all the way open.

They stepped inside. The house had been abandoned, obviously in a hurry. The drawers of the chest were open. Everything that signaled human habitation had been removed—towels, bric-a-brac, utensils.

But not one piece of furniture had been taken. A rolled-up runner near the door signified that the woman was in such a hurry to leave she had decided to leave the rug.

"She's gone. She's gone!" Didi was crushed.

"If she ever was here," Allie Voegler said.

Didi turned on him in a fury. He raised his hands high to signify that he was just joking. She moved away from him, trying to control her temper.

"I'm going to look around," she said.

"You mean search the premises?"

"Yes, that's what I mean."

"Well, you can do what you like. But I'm a

police officer. I don't conduct these kinds of searches without a warrant."

"Then wait outside," Didi retorted. "I surely don't want to get you in trouble."

Allie Voegler walked outside.

Didi went through the small gate house like a fury—prying and pulling and peeking. She investigated every nook and cranny.

Every time she caught a glimpse of Allie Voegler standing aloof outside, she increased her efforts.

But there was nothing to find, except for a ski hat, a long and somewhat tattered evening dress, a man's leather vest, and a small wooden jewel box.

It was such a strange-looking little box, dark wood with a brass clasp. It almost might have been a music box. She opened the lid half expecting some faint Chopin to emerge from within.

But she heard no music whatsoever. She did see several objects whose function she could not identify: three leather straps; narrow, weather-beaten, and each one a different length.

Pulling the straps aside, she saw, nestling at the bottom of the box, three sets of tiny silver bells. The first set was a cluster of two. The other two sets were clusters of threes. She picked one set up and rang them. A clear sweet sound of tinkling. She put it back down. Pretty but worthless. She closed the box and placed it with the clothes she had found and laid them all next to the rolled-up rug that Emily Matthiessen had left when she fled from the place.

Angry, confused, Didi slammed the door shut as she left, and joined a silent Allie Voegler in the car.

"Why don't you say something?" Didi demanded of her driving companion as they left.

"What do you want me to say?"

"You have that look on your face."

"What look?"

"I don't know. But it's not the look you had after I explained the crime-scene photos to you."

"Well, I'm a bit more skeptical now. I sort of fell hook, line and sinker for what you told me."

She asked sharply: "You mean you think I was lying about that woman? That she doesn't exist? That I fabricated her?"

"No. I don't mean that."

"Then you think I lied about what she told me: that she was Dick Obey's mistress and lover . . . and that Dick Obey was murdered."

Allie Voegler didn't respond for the longest time. He seemed to be trying to collect his thoughts, to present to her what he really believed.

Finally he said: "Look, what I believe really doesn't matter. What I'm going to do is this. When I get back to the office I'll write a report to my chief on what you told me about the photos and about the vanishing lady. He'll make the decision. If he decides it warrants an investigation, he'll order one. And he'll contact the State Police Homicide Division."

Didi squirmed in her seat. "Do you think he will order an investigation?"

"I don't know."

"But you're not going to recommend an investigation be started?" Her question was bitter.

"I will present what I know. I'm not a lawyer. I'm a police officer. I'm not an advocate for anyone."

"Hooray for you!" she exclaimed sarcastically.

He let it slide and concentrated on the road.

Didi sat at her desk in the small animal clinic. It was late afternoon. She had been out all day on rounds; a long, grueling day made more difficult by Charlie Gravis's surliness. He complained about everything, most of all the rheumy knee socket which continually tormented him.

It had been three days since her disappointing trip to Kent, Connecticut, with Allie Voegler. She had heard nothing. He hadn't contacted her. Was his report already on his chief's desk? Had it been ruled on? Why was there such a delay? Why hadn't anyone called to make inquiries about her analysis of the photos?

She was weary but on edge. She picked up her pad and flicked the switch to hear the day's telephone messages. Usual stuff—except for a message from the amorous gentleman farmer, Howard Danto, goat cheese maker extraordinaire. No, he wasn't calling to reaffirm his passion for her or to ask her out. He was calling to tell her that she should stop by Avignon Farms and ask for the foreman, Max. Howard Danto had recommended her to them. Danto ended his message by saying that he didn't know what would come of it . . . but she had nothing to lose.

Didi turned the machine off. My, that was nice of Howard Danto! Avignon Farms was one of the most important new thoroughbred horse-breeding facilities in Dutchess County. No, she had nothing to lose. Even the slightest foot in the door would be helpful.

It was hard for her to sleep that night. The face of that redheaded woman, Emily Matthiessen, kept appearing and dissolving. She couldn't get a fix on her. She remembered everything about that first visit . . . and virtually every word the woman said to her . . . but for some odd reason she couldn't remember the woman's face. Was it jealousy? The woman was very beautiful and she had claimed to be Dick Obey's lover, even mistress. Was that it? Had she wanted her own friendship with Dick Obey to be something more than friendship? Didi found this thought intolerable. She wasn't interested in older men. She was interested in finding a man near her own age; a man who wanted to do the same things she wanted to do. Didi was tired of being alone. She wanted someone to sleep with on the most profound as well as the most basic level.

She finally fell asleep, but when she awoke she was in a foul mood. She took a long, hot bath and left Charlie at the house, driving alone to the impressive Avignon Farms, about fifteen miles away.

It was a picture-book place—green, freshly painted buildings, snow-white fences, gravel driveways, and a small parking lot amidst landscape shrubs.

The foreman, Max, greeted her with a wave. He was standing in front of one of the large stables, chewing a small cigar. He was dressed like an old-fashioned horseman, even down to his knickers. His face was so lined it seemed that a harvester had rolled over it.

"Howard Danto told me to stop over," she said.

He tipped his peaked cap to her. "You the vet?" he asked. "Yes," Didi replied. Max shook hands with her. Then he looked her over, openly, without artifice. He smiled, but it wasn't a patronizing smile. He likes what he sees, Didi thought.

"Well," Max said, "here's the story. We use

Dr. Hull. But a lot of our horses go up to Saratoga in August for the racing season there. And Hull accompanies them. So we need someone to cover the stables down here, while he's up there."

Didi had heard of Dr. Hull. He had a long-established practice in Dutchess and Columbia counties, with strong ties to the downstate racing scene. This was a wonderful opportunity, she realized. It was truly a foot in the door.

"You been around racehorses a lot?" Max asked gently, his eyes now on a horse being led out of the barn to be shod.

"Yes," she replied quickly, "at Philadelphia Park."

It wasn't a lie but it wasn't the truth either. And the moment she replied, the damn memories flooded back—of Drew Pelletier, the young professor at veterinary school; the one who had seduced her and loved her and then dumped her; and broke her heart in the process. She had gone to the racetrack with him often, to help out. And once she had even worked with him on an insurance fraud case, where a racehorse had been murdered to collect on a big policy.

That memory jarred her almost as much as the memory of Drew. Why hadn't she told Allie Voegler that? It would have given her more legitimacy in his eyes. It would have made her appear somewhat experienced in criminal investigation.

Then Max stuck out his hand again. She shook it. He said: "Look, I got to work. Just call me the first week in July and we'll talk about schedules and fees. But meanwhile, why don't you just take a look around." She shook his hand and thanked him. He walked briskly toward the blacksmith who was setting up to work.

Didi walked into the large stable anchoring one end of the courtyard quadrangle. It was like walking into a church—a breathtakingly high ceiling . . . a long wide aisle between the stalls, which themselves seemed to be hand carved from mahogany. Serious-looking grooms moved in and out of the stalls, cleaning, currying, feeding. They just nodded at her. She had never seen such beautiful living quarters for horses.

She walked slowly down one side of the aisle, peering in at the horses. As she was about to make her turn at the end of the aisle, she heard a ferocious snort. She stopped and saw a pair of angry eyes glaring at her from the other side of the aisle—third stall down.

Didi walked there directly. It was a stallion—a lovely, finely made gray horse. He was full of himself—prancing a bit, shaking his head, alternately snorting and sticking out his lip.

She looked at the name tag on the outside of the stall. It read: JACK TOO.

Didi laughed, a bit astonished. She didn't know JACK TOO was standing at stud in Avignon Farms. She said to the gray horse: "Well, Jack, it's an honor to make your acquaintance." The horse snorted and shook his head vigorously. Didi surely knew the legend of JACK TOO.

He had run eighteen times and never won a race. But he had been second, seventeen times.

The fans grew to love him. If he was leading in a race, he would just slow down at the finish line so that another horse could pass him. He just refused to win. No one knew why. No one could change his style—to always come in second. JACK TOO, by the time he was sent to stud, had become one of the lions of equine eccentricity. But the horses he had sired since going to stud had won a great many times.

"Next time I visit, Jack, I'm going to bring you a whole bunch of carrots," Didi promised. JACK TOO reared up and tried to kick the stall down.

Didi drove straight home. It was rare that she was in the big house in the late morning. No one was around. Didi walked into the kitchen. A pot of coffee was, as usual, on the stove over a low light. She poured herself a third of a cup and sat down at the long table, leafing through the Hillsbrook newspaper that someone had left.

She stopped leafing at page six and stared at the photo of Trevor Brice.

The small headline read: LOCAL MAN ARRESTED.

The short paragraph beneath the headline said that Trevor Brice was arrested for criminal mischief—and released on bail. It is alleged, the paper went on to say, that Mr. Brice was on the property of the late Dick Obey just prior to the fire which destroyed the Obey farm. It is further alleged that actions by Mr. Brice at that time, while in an intoxicated state, contributed to the conflagration.

Angrily, Didi swept the paper onto the floor. If Allie Voegler believed that nonsense, there was no way he would open an investigation into Dick Obey's death. Why hadn't he had the manners to call her? Furious, she walked to the wall phone in the hallway and dialed the Hillsbrook Police. It took five minutes to locate Allie Voegler but Didi hung on tenaciously.

When his voice arrived, she asked, almost tauntingly: "Well, Officer Voegler . . . has there been any determination on Dick Obey?"

"I am afraid there has," he said. "I was going to call you."

"I'll bet you were," she said bitterly.

"My chief was unimpressed by the evidence," he explained.

"Your chief didn't even look at the photos. They're still in my office."

"It's no use," Allie Voegler said gently. "He won't budge."

"And you," she shouted into the phone, "will you budge?"

She hung the phone up in a fury. Then she strode into the clinic and stared at the sequence of gruesome photos still fastened to the light board. The images dissolved her anger in seconds. She started to cry. Then she heard someone in the kitchen. She desperately stifled her tears. She sat down at her desk and clenched her fists in front of her, like a schoolgirl. She would find out who murdered her friend all by herself.

Chapter Nine

Didi sat in her jeep for the longest time before she began the walk from the road to the Theobold farmhouse. She realized, in a sense, the absurdity of her position. She was about to dig. But the earth she was digging in consisted of the murdered man's friends. Dick Obey, in fact, as far as she knew, had had no enemies. Only friends and a beautiful mistress who had vanished. So, as ridiculous as it seemed, it was a friend who had murdered him . . . a friend who mutilated him . . . a friend who smeared the blood on his neck so carefully and then invited the dogs. She shivered even though the morning was warm. Was there still a sliver of life left in Dick Obey when the dogs went at him?

She tried to cheer up—penning a nonsense verse in her head . . .

He died in a ditch
near Delhi
Up to his neck in
redeye

It didn't cheer her up. She walked toward the house but stopped when she saw the barn doors open and the cows move slowly toward their morning pasture. A very small milking herd now.

Then she saw John and Helen Theobold standing close together by one of the barn doors, standing silently, watching the herd move off.

Didi felt a sudden surge of pride and affection for them as a couple—even though she really didn't know them very well. They just seemed the archetypal noble farm couple, standing there bravely in the midst of crumbling circumstances. And, Didi knew, their circumstances were truly crumbling. It was very hard to make a living producing milk. Helen had become an LPN and worked three nights a week in hospice care. John, himself, supplemented his farm income by hauling town garbage.

But standing there together, silently, watching the herd move off—they seemed to be fixed on the important things, on the eternal things: that they were man and wife and that they had survived. This was the kind of relationship that Dick Obey and his wife probably had—sturdy. She bit her lip. She was thinking like a fool. What about the redheaded woman?

John and Helen had spotted her. They waved. Didi walked quickly to them. "Morning! I was passing by, so I just thought I'd stop in and see how Bucket was doing," she lied.

Didi noticed that Helen had now slipped her arm loosely through the arm of her husband. She was a small, thin woman with very gentle eyes . . . "doe eyes" her mother used to call them. She was wearing a very old faded print dress, buttoned up to the collar.

"He's doing fine, that miserable dog," John Theobold said. "See for yourself." He whistled twice, strong piercing sounds.

Bucket came gallumping from one of the pastures. The moment he saw Didi he skidded to a stop so sharply he almost fell over.

"He doesn't like me anymore," Didi said.

"Get over here!" John Theobold ordered. Bucket sashayed over, rolling his eyes and twisting his neck in a submissive, guilty posture. The man reached down and pulled the hair away from the hot spot.

"See," he said, "it's almost all cleared up. Old Charlie Gravis's potion was just too much for Bucket. He doesn't even go near his leg anymore."

"Yes," Didi agreed, "it looks fine."

Theobold released Bucket, who sidled over to Helen for sympathy. She scratched him gently. Bucket groaned with pleasure.

There was an awkward silence. Then Didi blurted out: "Dick Obey was murdered!"

John Theobold's Lincolnesque face registered

shock. He took a quick step toward her and said: "Oh, Didi! I can't believe that. People around here loved Dick. You know that."

Didi shook her head. "I don't care who loved him or how wonderful he was. He was murdered."

"Did you go to the police?"

"Yes. They don't believe me."

Didi looked at Helen Theobold. The woman had kneeled and was hugging Bucket. She had the strangest look on her face, almost the trace of a smile. No, not a smile, just a kind of repose, as if recollecting something precious.

"It's wrong going around telling people things like this, Didi. It's just wrong," John Theobold gently chastised her.

"Wrong? What's wrong with telling the truth? And I'm beginning to realize, John, that Dick might not have been what he seemed."

"I don't understand you now."

"You know damn well what I'm saying."

"I won't speak disrespectful of the dead," he said. Then he turned to Helen. "Let's go back to the house."

"No, wait!" Didi pleaded. She was sorry she had snapped at him. The whole thing was going wrong. She looked at the kneeling Helen for help in placating her husband. But the woman was staring into the dog's eyes. When she finally did look at Didi, it was with great compassion, as if she knew Didi was suffering . . . and as if she understood that suffering. Then she stood up, took her husband's arm, and they both walked quickly back to the house. Bucket followed them.

Crushed, Didi walked slowly back to her jeep. This was not the way to conduct an investigation. But why had John Theobold acted so peculiarly? She was telling him the truth.

She sat in the jeep for a long time before starting the motor. Something else was bothering her dreadfully: the behavior of Helen Theobold. The moment the name Dick Obey had been mentioned the woman had gone into some kind of secret room and stayed there . . . as if she didn't want to hear any more . . . as if she were remembering something that could not be defiled.

Didi didn't want to think what she was thinking. But if Dick Obey had "kept" Emily Matthiessen . . . if those two had been lovers . . . then it was possible that Dick Obey had been Helen Theobold's lover also, at one time or another.

She turned the ignition key and headed toward Frank Draper's farm.

The farther away from the Theobold farm she got, the more she realized that the visit hadn't been as disastrous as she originally thought. Theobold wouldn't stay angry with her for long. She had simply forgotten that he was a religious sort who would be offended by any "disrespect" toward the dead. Besides, there was no way to find out anything important about Dick Obey's real life if she wasn't "disrespectful."

And there was Helen Theobold. That had been a revelation. *Something* had gone on between her and Dick Obey, although it was hard to say what . . . and it seemed that John Theobold was unaware of that connection, whatever it was. But husbands are always the last to know.

As she pulled into the Draper farm she reminded herself that she must not be interrogatory or confrontational. She must ask for help.

Frank Draper hailed her from one of his fields and signaled that he would meet her by the porch of the house in a short while. It was only the second or third time that Didi had been on the Draper farm. Frank kept no stock or animals, not even chickens; except for a house cat named Willie.

Didi sat down in the large wicker rocker on the porch and waited. She could see the three new pickup trucks Frank Draper had recently purchased to deliver his produce to New York City. He didn't use the regular distribution and wholesaling networks. He sold and delivered direct to the restaurants and his business had become one of the great success stories in the county.

An organic farmer making big money? It was unheard of. But Frank Draper had done it by growing vegetables that no one in Dutchess County had ever heard of, much less eaten. And he grew them on raised beds with a liberal use of portable sheds and plastic overheads, along with exotic natural fertilizers and luck. He was always being written up in the big city papers as the man who had popularized the Peruvian potato—a very small, deformed-looking blackish potato that Europeans had ignored for centuries. It was one of the most ancient, most nutritious, and when prepared correctly, one of the most delicious potatoes—and Frank Draper grew them and delivered them.

"And to what do I owe the honor of your visit?" Frank Draper asked, placing one foot on the porch and making a mock little bow while swinging his sweat-stained baseball cap in an arc.

There was something about Frank Draper she had always liked. He was younger than Dick Obey, and brasher, but he meant well, even though he often called her "honey." And he had the reputation of being a good friend to everyone. As people said: "Just don't get him drunk and don't get him angry." He was particularly generous with money. Half the people in Hillsbrook seemed to have borrowed money from him over the past five years—for everything from school tuition to barn repair to a second honeymoon. He never charged interest and he never pressed for payment. He disclaimed any unique generosity on his part, saying that he just hated banks and hated to see his friends have to borrow from them.

"How's your cat?" Didi asked.

"He's fine. He's even getting positively friendly. Yesterday he brought me a plump field mouse. I sautéed it and we both ate well."

He narrowed his eyes and then said: "You look a bit on edge, Didi. Everything okay?"

"No, Frank. Nothing is okay."

"Dick Obey?"

"Yes."

"I figured as much. You looked in bad shape when you came into the bar that day to tell us about Dick's lady friend." He paused, then added: "Dick's supposed lady friend."

"Frank," Didi replied, "I know Dick was murdered and I need your help. I need the help of all his friends because I can't get any from the Hillsbrook Police or the State Police, or anyone."

"Were you in love with him, Didi?"

She was taken aback by the question. "No! No. We just hung out together a lot. We used to talk to each other. And he helped me a lot."

Didi could tell he didn't believe her—not at all. He looked at his hands, turning them over. "You know, honey, Dick didn't drink a lot. I mean steadily. But he went on terrible binges and that's probably why it happened."

"I'm not saying he didn't get drunk in Dela-

ware County that night. I'm saying he was murdered while he was drunk."

"You mean he got into a fight in a bar there?"

"There was no report of any fight. Besides,
in my view it was a planned murder."

"What did the report say?"

"He was wandering drunk along the road late
at night and it happened. He collapsed or fell
asleep and the dogs got him. That's what the
report said. But I saw the pictures, Frank. I
studied them. Believe me, he was murdered."

His eyes drifted off. He seemed deep in
thought. Then Frank Draper said: "I always
wondered why so many dairy farmers become
alkies. They seem to drink more as they get
older. I think it's the cold. After forty, when
you're in muck every day, you just can't get
warm."

"You're changing the subject, Frank."

He laughed. "I guess I am, Didi. I just have
this funny feeling that what you're about now
is not murder but something you have to clear
up in your own mind about your friendship
with Dick."

"I am investigating a murder," she said stiffly.

"What are you using . . . the veterinary approach?" It was a sarcastic comment, but she
let it slide and just waited.

"So what do you want, Didi? Secrets about
Dick Obey? Okay. Secret Number One. When
I started this organic farming operation, Dick

was openly contemptuous. He said I was crazy, that it wouldn't work, that it was somehow beneath me. I got angry at him. But he ended up helping me out and not taking a penny for his work.

"Secret Number Two. Roger Brice once didn't speak to him for about six months because Dick testified in a criminal case against his son. This was years ago. But then Roger forgot all about it.

"Secret Number Three. George Hammond, the county agricultural agent—you know him—once had a fistfight with Dick. Some kind of political argument that got out of control. I think it was about Governor Cuomo. But two weeks later they were friends again.

"Secret Number Four. Every couple of years, in the summer, Dick used to get a bad case of hives."

He paused, scraped some dirt from the back of his hand, and then said: "And there may be a few more murderous secrets about, Didi. But that's all I could think of off the top of my head. Not really the stuff of murder, huh?"

"What about money, Frank?"

"What about it?"

"Was Dick as poor as people thought he was?"

"Worse."

"Then how could he pay rent for that woman in Kent, Connecticut?"

"You got me."

"It doesn't make sense," Didi said.

"It makes as much sense as these questions," Frank Draper replied, and for the first time Didi felt true hostility from him. She thanked him and left.

As she pulled away from Frank Draper's farm, she felt a sense of enormous futility. In fact, he had told her exactly what she wanted to hear . . . the dirty little secrets of Dick Obey's life. But they were ridiculous. Silly little arguments between friends . . . misunderstandings. No, that was not what she had meant . . . not what she was looking for. Then what?

Suddenly she grew very tired. She was used to taking care of sick animals and in that capacity she was tireless. But too much human interaction had always fatigued her.

She drove the jeep back home, went into her small animal clinic, and lay down on the examining table, only a few feet from the grisly photos of Dick Obey. In seconds she was fast asleep.

Noises woke her an hour later. Noises in the kitchen. But when she appeared suddenly, bleary-eyed, and, uncommonly, greeted Mrs. Tunney, Charlie, Abigail and Trent Tucker— Didi knew they had been talking or arguing about her and simply hadn't known she was sleeping in the small animal clinic. It wasn't a usual place for her to nap.

Trent Tucker defused the discomfort of the situation by happily telling the truth. He said: "We were just talking about you wandering around the town telling everyone Dick Obey was murdered."

Didi became furious for a moment but then relaxed and poured herself half a cup of coffee from the omnipresent pot. She should have known. In Hillsbrook, the gossip network was ruthless. If you fall down in the hardware store, a dairy farmer eleven miles away knows about it eleven minutes after it happens. Rural gossip—always there.

Mrs. Tunney glared at Trent Tucker, wiping her hands on her apron with such vigor that she almost ripped the fabric.

"Some people never know their place," she said, then turned and said sweetly to Didi: "I was telling them that righter words were never said. That man was not nice."

Didi didn't understand what she was talking about. "What man?"

"Dick Obey."

It was very odd. This was the first time she had ever heard a really bad word about Dick Obey and it was spoken right in her own kitchen.

"You mean you think he was murdered?" she asked Mrs. Tunney.

"Yes. I don't know by who. But yes. And you

know what happened to your mother. God rest her."

The mention of her mother's name was bewildering. Didi looked around, confused.

"I will tell you something we all never told a soul," Mrs. Tunney pronounced mysteriously, looking around at the others to confirm her long-time secrecy and the coming revelation.

"Oh, it was many years ago, when you first went off to college. Your mother caught Dick Obey poaching mourning doves in the pine forest. And you know what your mother did?"

Didi didn't answer. She just waited.

Mrs. Tunney gave an enormous sigh and answered her own question. "Nothing. God bless her. Your mother did nothing. She was a Christian woman. She forgave him. Yes, she just let it pass. She said poor Dick Obey was probably hungry and too ashamed to ask for help. It was when he lost his dairy herd."

Another dirty little secret, Didi thought, and this one infinitely more pathetic and nonsensical than the ones Frank Draper had revealed. Besides, she realized that everything Mrs. Tunney recounted from the past was suspect; the woman had a reputation for delusional thinking . . . too many pots of oatmeal stirred and served.

"Well," Didi said, scrupulously polite, "I thank you for that information, Mrs. Tunney. You can be sure I will be discreet with it."

Then Didi walked out of the house and toward the pine forest. Mrs. Tunney's tale had roused in her bittersweet memories of her mother. Yes, like Mrs. Tunney said, her mother had been a Christian . . . to a fault.

She stopped suddenly. No, she didn't want to go into the pine forest. She wanted to go back to work . . . to make her rounds.

She turned and saw Charlie Gravis waiting for her.

"I just wanted to say something to you, Miss Quinn."

"Yes, Charlie," she replied, trying to be polite again.

"Well, Miss Quinn, when I was a younger man I liked my drink. I surely did. And once or twice a month I used to like it *very* much. But when I really got the hankering to tie one on, I always went out of Hillsbrook. I mean, too many people know me in this town. I used to go one town over, or two towns. Or sometimes into Kingston or Rhinebeck or Fishkill."

He paused and waited. She didn't know how she was supposed to respond. She didn't know why he was telling her this nonsense.

"But," he continued, "I never went one hundred miles and two or three counties over. I never went to Delaware County to tie one on."

The sheer illuminating wisdom of what the old man said struck her so hard she brought her hands to her mouth, like a child surprised.

And then she realized what a fool she had been. It was such a simple contradiction!

What was Dick Obey doing so far away? Why go to Delaware County to get drunk? What, as the old country saying goes, was Charlie Smith's cow doing in Bill Jones's barn. It didn't belong there.

"We'll go to Delaware County in the morning, Charlie."

The old man nodded.

Chapter Ten

At dawn, they crossed the Hudson in the red jeep and drove west from Kingston, through Ulster and Delaware counties. It had been a long time since Didi had driven the winding Route 28 through those counties, and she reveled in the suddenly remembered towns—Woodstock, Roxbury, Phoenicia, Andes, Margaretville, and a host of others.

And once deep inside Delaware County they were in dairy cow country; much like Dutchess County was fifty years ago. The deeper they drove, the more rural the land became . . . the barns and the cows and the pastures seemed to move closer to the road, as if the road were a very new invention, dropped down from above to interfere with bovine existence.

Didi could sense Charlie Gravis's joy; the old dairy farmer hadn't seen so many cows since he was a young man. He just watched and purred.

Outside Delhi they reached the bar where Dick Obey had been drinking the night of his death. It was called, ridiculously, Town And Country.

"A damn general store," Charlie Gravis said with disgust as he stared at the dilapidated, low-to-the-ground, sprawling building, which seemed to sell just about anything you could want from condoms to shovels, but not in alphabetical order.

"How could someone get drunk in there?" Didi asked, shutting off the motor of the jeep.

"Well, Miss Quinn," Charlie reflected, "we all used to get drunk in general stores. One side of the store always had one of those low iceboxes. You take your beer from there, pay for it, then go outside, and someone always has a bottle of something stronger. Yes, Dick Obey sure could have got drunk in there, but who would travel all this way for this kind of drinking? It don't make sense. He just as well could have gone to the woods behind his barn. I mean, when I used to tie one on, I wanted to be in a beautiful bar. That's why I got out of Hillsbrook."

They walked inside. It was exactly as Charlie had predicted. The main store was a hodgepodge of everything from paint to underwear to sandwiches. And, on one side, along a wall, was an old-fashioned refrigerator case stocked with beer. Two young men were leaning against it drinking from cans. They seemed oblivious to the fact that it was early in the morning.

A girl of about seventeen was on a ladder, stacking bags of dried cat food.

Behind the counter was a tall, heavyset bald man with a large white apron, on which was stenciled the name of his establishment.

Didi walked over to him, Charlie following. She took out the obituary notice she had saved from the Hillsbrook paper and placed it on the counter.

"Morning, folks," the proprietor said cordially, but his eyes followed the piece of paper suspiciously.

"This man was a good friend of ours," Didi said, pointing to the picture that accompanied the obit. Her voice softened. "And we need your help."

The proprietor stared at the picture, then said: "I'm sorry. I never saw the man."

"But you do know him. He was in here the night he died."

He stared at the picture again. "Is this the man who died on the road?"

"Yes."

"Well, I told the State Troopers everything I knew about him."

"Tell me! Please! Was he drunk when he left?"

"I don't know. He had a few beers inside. Then he went out back. I know there were a few bottles of Wild Turkey out there. Always is." The proprietor folded his hands across his stomach. "You his daughter?" he asked.

"Just a friend," Didi replied.

"Well, I'm sorry about what happened. He was a nice guy. Never caused any trouble."

His last phrase startled Didi. Quickly she asked: "You mean he was in here more than once?"

"Oh sure. A couple of times a week."

Didi looked at Charlie almost accusingly. If Dick Obey had come here several times a week, then something else was going on—he wasn't just looking for a place to "tie one on" in obscurity.

"What did he talk about when he was here?" Didi pressed.

"Didn't talk much. Knew his place." The proprietor pushed the piece of paper back towards Didi. Didi started to say something, but he just wandered over to the two young beer drinkers, who were laughing hugely over some joke.

Didi and Charlie walked back to the jeep.

She climbed in and just sat there. Everything was getting more confusing.

"Why don't we get some breakfast?" Charlie Gravis suggested.

"I don't want breakfast," she snapped.

"Well, where do we go next?" Charlie persisted.

"I don't know."

Suddenly Charlie nudged her with his arm

and made a motion with his head toward the store.

Didi saw that the girl who had been stacking cat food was now standing in front of the store. She seemed to be in an agitated state, as if wanting to walk over to the car, but afraid to take the step.

Didi beckoned her over. The girl took two steps, then stopped. Didi smiled but didn't wave again. The girl would have to make it on her own, if she wanted to. What was she frightened of? Or was it just adolescent shyness?

When she finally reached the red jeep, there were tears in her eyes. "I just wanted to tell you how sorry I am. Mr. Fisk was the most generous man I ever met. It was a terrible thing."

Didi looked at the girl blankly, then at Charlie, then back to the girl. "Mr. Fisk?" she asked.

The girl stepped back. Her eyes widened. One hand nervously twirled a lock of her dirty blond hair. "Yes. Your friend. The man in the picture."

Didi pulled the obit out. "This man?" she asked the girl. The girl nodded. "But his name was Dick Obey," Didi explained.

The girl looked puzzled. "No," she said, "his name was Mr. Fisk. He stayed at the Sunshine Motel."

Then the girl seemed to realize that for some reason she had said quite enough. She turned without another word and walked back into the store.

Didi sat there dumbfounded. Why in heaven would Dick Obey use a fake name? What was he doing at a motel? What did the girl mean by his "generosity"? Was Dick Obey also giving gifts to teenage girls? Had he tried to seduce her?

"At least," Charlie Gravis said laconically, "we know where we're going next."

They found the Sunshine Motel close to the Delaware-Otsego County line.

At first glance it was a dismal, rickety place—just a long, low structure with twenty-four doors opening onto a weedy courtyard.

But the motel was set in a glorious field filled with wildflowers and framed by groves of high trees.

Three cars were parked in the lot. It was obviously not boom season for the Sunshine Motel.

Didi and Charlie parked the jeep in front of the office and walked inside.

A skinny young man dressed in an outdated suit with an enormous tie was behind the desk, reading a newspaper and listening to a radio talk show.

Didi hesitated for just a moment. She had to establish authority and credibility.

She winced when she realized that she was

evaluating this young man much as she would evaluate a horse in a stall she was about to enter.

The young man greeted them with a smile. He had a button on his jacket lapel that read: I'M JONAH.

Didi dropped her American Express card on the counter flamboyantly and began to spin out a fanciful tale.

"We need two rooms for a couple of nights. I'm a veterinarian from Albany. This is my assistant. We're down here to do some testing—tick infestations."

Jonah smiled. Didi added a flourish: "I hope everything is working in the rooms. We have to set up a couple of lap top computers and a fax machine."

"No problem," Jonah assured her, selecting two keys from the wall board and starting to do the paperwork.

"Thirty-one dollars per night per person," he said.

"Fine!" Didi replied.

Now, she thought, now is the time to strike. "Your place was recommended to us," she said.

"By who?" Jonah asked, not even looking up from his labors and obviously just asking out of politeness.

"Dick Fisk," she said, matter-of-factly.

The young man reacted as if he had been

punched in the stomach. He dropped his pen and stood straight up.

"Wasn't that horrible! What happened to Mr. Fisk! Just when everything was going so good for him. You know, let me tell you something. He never came in here drunk. And we used to talk a lot."

Jonah feverishly pulled out his wallet and extracted a business card. He handed it to Didi. She looked at it carefully, trying to remember every detail.

It read: Dick Fisk
           GOOD ACREAGE REALTY INC.
           P.O. Box 1183
           Albany, New York 12227

Jonah took the card back and began to tap it in his hand.

"Mr. Fisk gave me this. He told me that I could have a job with his company in the fall. And then he just died. Just like that. Just when he hit the jackpot."

"What jackpot?" Didi asked quietly, beginning to get nervous that the young man would become suspicious of two strangers asking questions about a dead man. But Jonah desperately wanted to speak. He had obviously really thought he would get a job with Dick Fisk, and he had obviously been deeply affected by his death.

"The farms! Those dairy farms he bought about six months ago. It was all going good. Three in a row. He bought old man Vernon's farm. And then Waverly Secor sold. And then Sid Hand."

Didi and Charlie looked at each other in astonishment.

It was Charlie Gravis who asked simply: "Local farms?"

"Sure. Right down the road from here. Off Route Twenty-eight. Past the landfill."

The young motel clerk was getting more and more upset. He shut off the radio in a fury.

"Mr. Fisk said everything had fallen into place. Things were breaking for him, he said. Luck was good. There was no problem. The farms had been vacated. Old Man Vernon died right after he got the money. And Secor moved to Vermont. Only Sid Hand is still around here. He bought a mobile home in Mount Vision. Everything was going good. And then boom. Mr. Fisk dies like that."

Jonah looked at Didi as if he expected some kind of spiritual or philosophical help from her. She said nothing. Jonah did the remaining paperwork with a trembling hand and gave Didi the keys.

"Let's just walk into the rooms," Didi said to Charlie. He nodded dutifully. They inspected each motel room, ritually trying the lights and plumbing.

Then they walked slowly back to the jeep. Everything was breaking too fast for Didi. Too many new things. New symptoms. New names. She had to go slowly . . . to keep her eyes on the prize . . . to keep her head clear.

They drove past the landfill to see the purchased farms. Already the buildings were beginning to decay. The entrances were wired shut with No Trespassing signs. Didi then pulled the jeep off the road and found Mt. Vision on the map—a small hamlet in Otsego County located between Oneonta and Cooperstown.

"Okay, Charlie," she said, folding the map with precision, "we can get something to eat now."

They ate lunch at a lovely health food restaurant in Oneonta called the Autumn Cafe. Charlie grumbled at the selection but finally settled on a vegetarian "hamburger."

After ordering, Charlie sat back and pronounced: "I think, Miss Quinn, we are opening a dangerous can of worms."

"Worms don't come in cans," Didi retorted.

"And I think we ought to go easy."

Didi tapped her spoon lightly on her glass. Charlie was right, she knew. This might lead anywhere. After all, she knew it had already led to murder.

"What do you want me to do, Charlie? Go to the police? I already went to the police."

They ate the meal in silence and then went looking for the small trailer park in Mt. Vision—a fifteen-minute drive from Oneonta.

They found it quickly, on a patch of sparsely wooded land off County Road 14.

Only four mobile homes were hooked up; each one more decrepit than the other. Each of the homes had a sign in front with the identity of the occupant.

The HAND sign was brightly painted.

Didi pulled the jeep right up to the mobile home.

Two children sat together on the steps staring at them.

A man and a woman were weeding a vegetable garden on one side of the trailer.

"Are you Sid Hand?" Didi asked from the jeep.

The man gave her an ugly look and didn't answer. The woman didn't even look up. They were both young—about Didi's age. And they both had that wolflike look that signals hard times.

"I'm not a bill collector, Mr. Hand," Didi assured him.

It was the woman who finally spoke: "What do you want?"

"I just want to talk to you about Dick Fisk, the man who bought your farm."

The man and woman exchanged glances. Didi could sense tension between them—not solidarity in the presence of a threatening stranger.

"Well, Mr. Hand, if you won't talk about the man who bought your farm . . . why don't you just tell me why you sold. We passed it this morning. A lovely piece of property. And it looked like a going concern."

"Who the hell are you?" the man asked bitterly.

Before Didi could answer, Mrs. Hand began to laugh. Then she began to yell at her husband. "Go ahead! Show her! Show her what a fool you were. Show her why you sold everything—the land, the herd, the machinery—for peanuts!"

"Shut up!" Mr. Hand barked.

The woman laughed again and walked into the trailer. She came right back out holding what seemed to be a photograph and thrust it triumphantly into Didi's hand.

It was a garish, reproduced color photograph of a milk cow in a milking shed.

The photograph had been taken from the rear and graphically recorded a very bad and very advanced case of the disease mastitis.

The animal's udders were swollen, discolored, grotesque in their infirmity.

Suddenly the man leaped forward, reached over the door of the open jeep, and snatched the photo from her hand.

His wife began to scream at him. "Go ahead!

What are you ashamed of? Show her the photo. Let her look at it."

Mr. Hand ripped it into shreds.

"Get out of here!" he threatened. "I don't know who you are or why you're here but I want you away from here!" He picked up a shovel.

"Let's get moving," Charlie whispered to her. She didn't need any encouragement. She started the jeep and they drove off.

"Getting stranger all the time," Charlie said as they headed back into Delaware County.

Didi didn't answer. She was thinking about that photograph. It was oddly familiar. Somewhere, she had seen it before, or something like it.

It was vague in her head but it was real and important. It was somehow the linchpin of the whole mess, she realized. Of the murder . . . of Dick Obey's secret life . . . of Good Acreage Realty. And she knew someone who could help her sort it out. Yes, she surely did.

"We're going back to the motel to turn in the keys and then we're going back to Hillsbrook," she informed Charlie.

"About time," was all he could say.

Chapter Eleven

Didi sat on her mother's bed, feverishly searching through a collection of her old phone books and slips of loose paper on which she had written various numbers. She was furious with herself. How could she have lost or mislaid the office number of Hiram Bechtold? He had been her favorite teacher in veterinary school. When her fury abated, she stared gloomily out into the night. There were neither stars nor moon visible; only a wispy fog.

Then she realized that she could easily get his home number from Information and call him there now rather than wait until morning. He lived in Narbeth, a small village in Lower Merion Township, just outside Philadelphia.

She got the number quickly, then tried to relax for a few minutes before calling. It had been a very long day what with all that driving; all those conversations; all those cryptic revelations. But she had napped when she got back and eaten a pot roast sandwich which Mrs.

Tunney had left in the refrigerator for her with Didi's name penciled rather crudely on it.

It really wasn't the fatigue that was making her feel less than completely functional. It was the constant excitement and stress of this peculiar search . . . or investigation . . . or whatever it was.

She called Philadelphia Area Information and quickly got the number. She dialed. Hiram Bechtold answered and the moment she heard that gruff but kindly voice she felt a surge of nostalgia for her school days.

"It's Didi Nightingale," she announced.

"Well, it's about time you called, Miss Nightingale," Hiram said, "I had heard you were lost in the wilds of New York State."

She laughed, happy, so happy to hear his voice again. They chatted for a few minutes about the school, about his family, about her practice.

Then she described the photograph she had seen while visiting Sid Hand.

She described it in detail, taking her time, trying to reconstruct it exactly for her old professor.

Before she had even finished the description, Hiram Bechtold burst out laughing.

"I know it, Didi! And I know where it comes from. In fact, young lady, I'm old enough to have been raised on those kinds of pictures."

"Raised on them?" Didi repeated, not understanding his phrasing.

"Let me explain. In the nineteen twenties and thirties, before there was rigorous hands-on training for both medical and veterinary students—the textbooks were much more graphic. If a medical student wanted to see what a case of advanced paretic syphilis looked like, he didn't have access to wards. Instead, he just opened a textbook that had graphic photos of that disorder. When a vet student wanted to see an advanced case of mastitis in cows, he also opened a textbook. And I'm sure the photo you saw was probably reproduced from one of the most famous textbooks of that time—*Bovine Disease* by Ariel."

Didi listened with awe as her old professor illuminated the origin and use of the photo. He hadn't slowed down at all.

"But why would one dairy farmer show that old photo to another dairy farmer?" she asked. Then added: "Or a real estate man to a potential customer?"

Hiram Bechtold laughed.

"Whoever showed it," he speculated, "may have just had a sick sense of humor. Or maybe your dairy farmer wanted to frighten the hell out of the other dairy farmer. It's a very ugly photo."

The word he used—"frighten"—made her sit up straight.

It was like an alarm clock going off in her head.

The photo, she realized, could have been a weapon. Yes, a weapon! A threat. An extortion. She clutched the phone tightly. Her imagination was beginning to race.

For the first time since this whole mess started, she could see the contours of a criminal scheme.

Excitedly, she asked: "Who would have access to that textbook now?"

He laughed. "Didi, there are probably thousands of old dog-eared copies of that book still around, in old trunks. But to find a copy good enough to make good reproductions—I guess you'd have to look in a specialized library. A vet school library, maybe. I have a mint copy. Sometimes I look through it and laugh. We've come a long way since then."

"Can you send me your copy?" she leaped in.

"It's a fat book, Didi."

"Just send it to me Federal Express in the morning. I'll mail you back whatever the postage."

She realized that she was literally pleading with him and she felt stupid, but she had to have that book.

"Didi, you are acting strange. But sure, I'll send it if you want it. And meanwhile, when are you going to pay us a visit in Philadelphia? You can give a talk. Very few of our graduates ever establish their own practice so quickly."

"Soon," she said, "soon." She couldn't make any more small talk. She said she had to go. She hung up.

It was becoming cold in the room and Didi wrapped herself in Dick Obey's serape.

Then she sat at her mother's desk and wrote the name and address of Dick Obey's real estate company that she had memorized from the business card shown to her by the motel clerk.

She stared at her own writing. She shivered. It had been a long time since she felt this kind of intellectual excitement—not since she had treated her first patients in the clinic at the vet school.

Then she ripped the sheet off the pad and walked quickly downstairs, through the darkened kitchen and into the "servants" quarters.

Only then did she hesitate, realizing that Charlie was probably fast asleep . . . and that it was an unwritten law that *their* part of the house was off limits to *her*. Damn protocol, she thought. I own this house. I feed them.

There was no light under Charlie Gravis's door but she knocked anyway.

He opened it just a sliver, bleary-eyed, and said: "Just a minute, Miss Quinn. I'll get my bathrobe." Five seconds later he was back, saying: "I don't have a bathrobe." He opened the door and Didi walked in. Charlie was wearing a pair of very washed-out long johns.

She handed him the paper briskly.

"Charlie, I want you and Trent Tucker to drive to Albany early tomorrow morning in the jeep. I want you to find out who was in business with Dick Obey. This may be a post office box alone, or it may be one of those commercial mail drops. But you find out. Dick used the name Fisk but one of the names had to be legitimate in order to register as a business with the County Clerk up there. Just find out!"

Charlie looked very sad. But he didn't argue with the request . . . maybe because she had made it clear that it was an order.

"Now you go back and get some sleep," she said, as kindly as possible.

Just as she was walking back into the hallway, out of his very small room, she saw the shotgun in the corner.

Furious, she wheeled and said: "I thought I told you, Charlie, that I didn't want any shooting on the property. Not deer . . . not woodchucks . . . not crows . . . nothing!"

"Just cleaning it, Miss Quinn," Charlie mumbled, "just cleaning it."

Didi gave him a hard look and then strode into the kitchen, turned on the light, and went to the refrigerator. All this excitement had made her hungry again. She knew she was about to find the person who had murdered and mutilated her friend. It was a triumphant hunger.

Chapter Twelve

It was a long 36-hour wait for an anxious Didi.

The book from Hiram Bechtold arrived first—at eight in the morning. And Didi excitedly ripped open the wrapper in the kitchen, in front of an astonished Mrs. Tunney and Abigail.

She opened the book to the page marked by her professor. Yes! That was the photograph!

The other package, Charlie Gravis, arrived forty minutes later, along with Trent Tucker.

"Give an old man a cup of coffee," he said to Mrs. Tunney, and sat down at the table.

"How did it go?" Didi asked.

"I got what you want. It was hard. But I got what you want."

"Thank you, Charlie. But I already knew who it was."

"You knew? If you knew, Miss Quinn, why would you send me up there?" Charlie asked, confused and a bit petulant.

"To confirm, Charlie." Didi picked up the

131

book from the table. "It's George Hammond, isn't it, Charlie?"

"Well, I'll be damned! How did you know, Miss Quinn?"

"Come along, Charlie, and I'll show you."

"What about my coffee?"

"Leave it!"

She drove to the Hillsbrook police station and left Charlie in the jeep when she walked inside. Allie Voegler was standing against a wall of the trailer reading a paper.

She walked over to him. He was so engrossed he didn't notice her. She tapped him on the shoulder. He saw her. He appeared startled.

"Could you spare me about thirty minutes?" Didi asked.

"For what?"

"I want to deliver to you Dick Obey's murderer."

"That's nice of you," he said sarcastically.

She just stood there.

"Okay. Listen. Is this some kind of joke? I don't have time for jokes."

"No joke," Didi said. She could see he was evaluating her again . . . as to her sanity. Then he said wearily: "Sure, Madame Vet, anything you want. Lead the way."

As they exited the trailer, Didi motioned to Charlie that he should get out of the jeep.

The three of them then walked down the main street of Hillsbrook to the old red stone building that anchored the north end of the street and was home to three lawyers, two insurance agents, and the County Agricultural Extension Service, which took up half of the lower floor.

Didi opened the glass door. George Hammond was stacking new pamphlets on the wall shelf. Then he tacked one of the pamphlets onto the enormous cork bulletin board that announced meetings and workshops for farmers in the area and displayed reports from various state agricultural projects.

The moment Hammond saw her and her companions, his face broke into a smile. He was a handsome man, a bit stooped, with farmer hands. He always wore a starched shirt and tie with suspenders. His clean-shaven face was always nicked, a little dot of blood visible on his cheek.

"I've been meaning to call on you, Didi," he said. "I think I've found a good replacement for the rabies committee."

Didi didn't reply. Hammond then shook Allie Voegler's hand and greeted Charlie Gravis.

"May I use your library for a minute?" Didi asked, a bit theatrically.

"That's what it's there for," George Hammond replied, gesturing toward the corridor that led to the library.

"I'll be back in a minute," she said. "Charlie,

do me a favor. Go back to the jeep and bring that book in here."

Charlie nodded and left. Didi waited until he was out of the door before heading toward the library. It was necessary that there be no confusion as to the sequence of events. It was necessary that Allie Voegler know she went into George Hammond's library empty-handed; that she had left her copy of *Bovine Disease* in the jeep.

Didi entered the library. Her legs and hands were tingling from the excitement. The whole case depended on what she found here. She had figured that Charlie Gravis would discover that George Hammond was the silent partner in the realty company. She had known that with some degree of certainty immediately after her conversation with Hiram Bechtold . . . when the first dim contours of a criminal conspiracy became clear to her. Such a conspiracy, no matter how brilliant, could not be pulled off without documents, seals, authoritative letters. And Dick Obey knew only one man who could provide them—County Agent George Hammond.

She reached the shelf line. The books were arranged alphabetically by title. She wouldn't even have to walk into the stacks. There it was—*Bovine Disease*.

She pulled it down, cradled it in her arms, and headed back toward the office. She cautioned herself against any display of flamboyance. This was not a lecture hall . . . this was a murder case.

The moment George Hammond saw Didi emerge with the book, he sat down at his desk. Didi noted with satisfaction that the color had drained from his face.

Allie Voegler appeared confused. Charlie Gravis had brought the other copy of the book from the jeep, so now both he and Didi held seemingly identical copies of the book.

Then Voegler said to Didi: "I am getting weary of your games. Isn't it time you made some sense?"

Didi replied, extravagantly: "You have been most kind, Officer Voegler, so now I am going to repay that kindness. I'm going to make you a local hero . . . the man who arrested Dick Obey's murderer."

Then she dropped the book onto the desk. She looked at Hammond as she spoke, but her words were directed to Voegler.

"It was really a very old scam. George Hammond formed a realty company in Albany. He hired Dick Obey as his front man. Obey went into Delaware County, called on dairy farmers and offered them ridiculously low prices for their land. The farmers refused to sell. So Dick Obey then showed them a picture. Charlie, please open your book to the marker and show Officer Voegler the photograph."

Charlie did as he was told.

Didi continued: "Ugly, isn't it? Now, where did Dick get that photograph? Take a look here, Officer Voegler." She tapped the copy of the book on the desk, the one she had taken from Hammond's library. Allie Voegler walked quickly to the desk and opened the book to the corresponding page. This was the moment of truth.

"It's gone," he said. "Someone ripped it out."

Didi felt a surge of triumph. "No," she replied, "someone *cut* it out carefully so that it could be easily and faithfully reproduced. George Hammond cut it out and reproduced it. Dick Obey circulated it to the dairy farmers. He told them, no doubt, that a terrible contagion of mastitis was sweeping Dutchess County but had been hushed up. He probably showed them a confirming letter on the county agent's stationery. He probably told them the contagion was spreading west and it would be crazy not to sell now because in six months all the milk herds in Delaware County would be decimated. He is persuasive. He speaks their language. The photo is frightening and authentic. The letter from the county agent confirming the contagion is official looking. The farmer sells. Hammond and Obey have obtained a prime piece of real estate for one-tenth of what they should have paid."

Didi paused. She wanted a glass of water.

George Hammond had swiveled around on his chair, looking away from her. Allie Voegler was listening to her, rapt.

"Then," she continued, "something happened. I don't know what. Dick Obey must have wanted more money or threatened to expose the scam. After all, he needed more and more money to keep his beautiful young woman happy. So, his demands probably became too much to bear. George Hammond hired Trevor Brice to murder him and fake an accidental death from drunkenness and stray dogs . . . and then burned Obey's farm to the ground to make sure all evidence of Good Acreage Realty was destroyed."

She was finished. There was absolute silence in the room. Then Allie Voegler leaned over the desk and asked George Hammond gently: "Is what she says true, George?"

Hammond's face was like a death mask now . . . as if parchment had been drawn over the bones. One hand kept plucking at his suspenders. He tried to rise but couldn't. Then he said in a hoarse whisper: "I didn't kill him, Allie, believe me. I didn't kill him." He kept repeating it.

Didi walked out. Charlie followed, clutching the nonmutilated copy of *Bovine Disease* tightly. Once they were in the jeep, Didi kicked angrily at the floorboard. "I wanted to see him put the handcuffs on Hammond." She seemed about to rush back in to satisfy her desire, then thought better of it and started the engine.

"Coffee, Charlie?" she asked.

"That would be nice," Charlie agreed.

Chapter Thirteen

Mrs. Tunney picked up the linen napkin and felt its weight. Charlie Gravis stared at the enormous goblet of water. Abigail looked to be in shock. Trent Tucker kept writhing in discomfort from the unaccustomed suit.

No one seemed to be happy but Didi—and she was *very* happy. She was celebrating, and that's why all five of them were seated in one of the poshest restaurants in Dutchess County. She had solved the murder of her friend and was buying her "retainers" dinner. It was noblesse oblige.

The waiter came with the champagne and filled their glasses.

"A toast to Charlie Gravis, whose help was invaluable," Didi said. Everyone drank except Abigail. Alcohol gave her a bad rash.

Then Didi made a toast to the memory of Dick Obey. "He would be very proud of us," she said. They all drank again, seemingly having forgotten that if Didi's analysis was correct, Dick Obey had been the crassest kind of thief.

Then Didi ordered for all of them. The food came in waves and after an initial period of puzzlement at the names and shapes of the strange dishes Didi's companions dug in and ate. Charlie, in fact, had two orders of mussels meunière.

When dessert came, a thoroughly tipsy Charlie Gravis told how Didi had confronted George Hammond in his office. His retelling of the event had no bearing on reality. It sounded mythical, heroic, dramatic . . . especially when, according to Charlie, Didi had slammed down the copy of *Bovine Disease* onto Hammond's desk with such force that it sounded like a gunshot.

By the time the celebratory dinner was over, no one was fit to drive, except Abigail, so she drove them all home.

Didi said good night, climbed the stairs and fell fully clothed onto the bed. She had never felt so good or so tired. She wished for a moment that the woman who claimed to have been Dick Obey's lover had been at the dinner.

And then she fell asleep.

The next morning the Hillsbrook paper had a small story with the headline—COUNTY AGENT SUSPECT IN LAND SCAM. It briefly told of land speculation and shenanigans in Delaware County. It said Hammond was a suspect because his name was linked to one of the realty companies involved.

It made no mention of Dick Obey or his murder.

"It takes a few days to get a murder indictment," Charlie explained.

Didi wondered whether she would be called as a witness before a grand jury. She wondered if Hammond had already confessed the murder. She wondered if Trevor Brice had indeed been the actual murderer, on Hammond's instructions.

"Do you feel okay, Charlie? You had a lot of champagne last night. You want to take the day off?" Didi asked.

"I'm ready to work," Charlie retorted, almost pugnaciously.

Off they drove in the red jeep—Dr. Nightingale and her trusted assistant.

Four days after the confrontation in Hammond's office, as Didi was doing her morning yoga, she saw Allie Voegler's car pull around the back of her house.

She stopped her exercises and smiled. She knew why he was here. To apologize. To eat crow. To say he was sorry that he doubted her and her theory.

Didi stood up. She was determined to be gracious . . . not to rub it in. After all, she was a trained scientist. She wondered what he had told his fellow police officers about her role in the case . . . how much credit he had taken for himself and how much he'd given her.

She walked halfway to the car and waited for him to join her. But he didn't get out of the car. He just slid to the far window and called out: "Good morning."

How prosaic, she thought. "Good morning," Didi replied.

The moment she saw the slight smirk on his face she realized that she had misinterpreted this visit.

"I'm afraid your case has collapsed," he said.

"What do you mean—collapsed?" she burst out angrily.

"Well," he said laconically, "it was kind of sloppy police work. But you're a vet, not a cop. Hammond gave us a full confession. You were right that there was a scam involving the photo. Hammond set it up and hired Obey because there was a rumor that Toyota was going to buy huge tracts of land off Route Twenty-eight in Delaware County for an assembly plant."

"Get to the point," Didi said angrily. "I know there was a scam. And a murder."

"But the scam turned out to be a disaster. Their company is bankrupt. Toyota decided not to build there. Hammond and Obey were left holding the bag. A lot of useless farm land. And all Dick Obey got for his troubles was six hundred dollars. Now, I ask you. How could anyone support a beautiful Connecticut woman on that? And why would anyone murder Dick Obey over useless land that was about to be taken over by the bank—because Hammond's firm was collapsed."

Didi felt weak, very weak. She walked over to the hood of Voegler's car and leaned against it.

"It was a good try," Allie Voegler said in his most patronizing manner. "And Hammond will be fired for his scam. But he has an alibi for the night Obey died. And there's absolutely no evidence that Trevor Brice was involved with either of them. So, Miss Nightingale, we're right back where we started. Aren't we? The coroner was right. The State Troopers were right. Dick Obey got drunk, fell into a ditch, passed out, and the dogs got him. That's all."

He started the engine. Didi, dazed, stepped away from the car.

"Maybe we can have a cup of coffee together sometime," he said jauntily, then drove off.

Didi walked slowly into the house, pale, her fists clenched. Wordlessly, she walked past the four breakfasters in the kitchen and entered the clinic area. She put the crime-scene photos back up on the illuminated board.

The ravaged face and body of her friend were like a personal attack on her . . . on her failure. Her anger flared as she studied them again. He was murdered. She believed it still. He was murdered. She wanted to break something. She wanted to smash Allie Voegler in the face.

Then she caught her breath. "Calm down, girl," she whispered to herself. "Calm down. You lost. It's all over."

A wave of fatigue came over her. Yes, she realized once and for all, it's all over.

Calmly, she took down the photos one at a time. She would hide them in a safe place. She would finally bury Dick Obey.

Chapter Fourteen

Summer came to Dutchess County with a vengeance in mid-July. The air was heavy with
heat. The pace slowed for Didi. She read a lot.
She took long rides alone in her jeep to the
historical sites and parks of Dutchess County;
including stately mansions and arboretums and
Revolutionary War battlefields and wineries.
She ordered new veterinary books. She contemplated a shopping trip to Manhattan.

As the summer progressed, her large animal
work began to slow and her small animal work
grew. In her clinic she treated dogs with heat
stroke from being left in cars; house cats dehy-
drated from two days of wilding; canaries who
had simply collapsed in their cages; goldfish
with dropsy; and a box tortoise inundated by
house paint.

It was on the third Sunday of July, after her
retainers had left for church together, which
they always did around 9:45 A.M., that Didi decided to drive into Columbia County. Her goal

was quite specific: to purchase cherry and rhubarb pies at Hoskin's Farm Market, the wonderful place Didi's mother used to drive up to once a month. It was a working farm that allowed customers to pick their own vegetables and fruit. But it was also famous for its pies, and Didi now longed for one with the same intensity that she had when she was a child and knew her mother had one in the house.

Didi first drove west and then turned north, up River Road 9 and then into 9G. She slipped her new cassette into the player. It was a tape of an old folk singer named Van Ronk she had found in the music store. Her roommate at vet school had once told her about him. The first song was okay, but the second was that old blues number "St. James Infirmary," and when she heard the line . . . *So cold, so pale, so still* . . . Didi burst into tears for no reason whatsoever. Then she just calmly drove along the Hudson and listened to the music as the river breezes washed over the open jeep.

When she reached Hoskin's Farm she was shocked by the changes that had taken place there. The sheds had become a store. The butter and cheese were now displayed in individual containers like one finds in a supermarket. The pies were now covered with plastic wrap. She realized then that it had been almost ten years since she had last been here, with her mother. A long time ago.

She purchased six pies, some jars of quince jelly, three dozen brown eggs, and, for some reason, an apron.

She loaded it all into the jeep and headed back home, happy. She put some Patsy Cline on.

She was so lost in the music on the trip home that she didn't even see the two Hillsbrook police cars parked in front of her property until she actually pulled in beside them.

Then she saw Trent Tucker trotting toward her. He was shaking his head from side to side.

"What's going on?" Didi asked as he reached the jeep.

"Someone broke into your clinic when we were at church. Damn! What a mess!"

Didi walked quickly into the clinic office. Trent Tucker followed. Two uniformed officers greeted her. She didn't know them at all.

"It looks like the thief broke in through the back. Busted a window . . . opened a latch," said one of the officers.

Didi was horrified. The place had been trashed. Drawers flung open and emptied. Files strewn wildly about. Supplies ripped apart. Her wall drug cabinet had been cracked open—they hadn't even bothered trying to force the lock. Chairs and tables were kicked over.

She righted a chair and sat down. Her retainers hovered about, clucking, not knowing what to do.

Then Allie Voegler entered. He spoke briefly with the two uniformed officers, nodded to Didi, and began to look around.

"He was after the drugs," Allie announced. "And it looks like he got them."

Didi didn't reply. She was in shock. "Would you like some cold juice?" Mrs. Tunney asked her in a motherly fashion. Didi shook her head no. She stared at the splintered wood of the drug cabinet. It was obvious that the thief had taken everything, indiscriminately: the Bute, the Lasix, the pain killers, the muscle relaxers; even the worming medicines which she had always kept in the drug cabinet for no good reason whatsoever.

"We're going to need a list of the drugs that were taken," she heard Allie Voegler say to her in an officious voice. She nodded. The two uniformed policemen were walking around with small kits, starting to dust for fingerprints.

Allie Voegler said: "Did you hear me, Dr. Nightingale? We'll be needing a list." She noticed that he had started calling her "Doctor" all the time. "Okay! Okay!" she replied angrily, stood up and walked to the desk, which for some reason had escaped the wrath of the thief. She opened the top right drawer. The pharmaceutical order sheets were there, untouched.

"I'll give it to you tomorrow," she said.

"Fine," Allie Voegler replied.

Didi sat down behind the desk and waited

for the Hillsbrook Police Department to finish its investigation. The officers took another thirty minutes to complete their tasks, and during that time no further word was spoken between Allie and Didi. After they were gone, Abigail and Trent Tucker righted the furniture and started to clean up the mess.

"Let's do this tomorrow," Didi said, and they both vanished, leaving Didi all alone in the mess. She remembered the pies in the jeep but she was too weary to get them. This kind of stuff—breaking and entering—was something she expected in Philadelphia when she lived there, but not in Hillsbrook.

She felt exhausted. She needed a nap. She started to leave but then realized the pharmaceutical sheets should be put in a safe place—and nowhere in this clinic seemed safe anymore.

She took them into the kitchen and opened the enormous parrot cage.

This was where Didi's mother had always kept her valuable papers—under the oilcloth at the bottom of the cage. She had figured that no thief would think of looking there . . . and if they did, they would have to face the wrath of Hope and Charity. It was a tradition Didi had maintained. The parrot cage, now empty of parrots, had become her safe deposit vault also.

Didi picked up the oilcloth to insert the papers.

She stepped back. Startled.

The brown envelope with the photos of Dick Obey was gone. She remembered distinctly that this was where she had put them.

Didi ripped the entire oilcloth out. No. The envelope was gone!

She turned, walked quickly through the hallway, up the stairs and into her bedroom, and flung herself onto the bed. Her mind was racing. She turned onto her stomach, then onto her back. She got off the bed and flung all the windows wide open. She lay down again. She got up and tried the window fan. It was still not fixed. She flopped down on one of the easy chairs.

Why would anyone steal those photos? How would anyone know they were there? Did the thief who broke into the clinic steal them? How could that be? It didn't make sense. He was after drugs. Besides, why would he rummage around the bottom of an old, empty bird cage in a different room of the house?

She got up and started to pace.

A bizarre possibility emerged. What if the thief had committed the robbery of the drugs and the trashing of her clinic just to cover up the theft of the photos?

And then she thought of something quite logical and quite terrible, so terrible she sat back down.

The only people who knew that the cage was

used as a safe deposit vault were Mrs. Tunney, Charlie Gravis, Abigail, and Trent Tucker.

Had one of them robbed the cage and destroyed the clinic as a cover?

Had one of them participated in Dick Obey's murder and wanted the photographs destroyed?

The logic played itself out. Supposedly they were all in church at the time. They all had alibis. But if one vanished from the church service, none of the others would tattle on him or her.

What was going on?

Didi didn't want to think these thoughts. They were too ugly.

She rushed downstairs into her clinic to photocopy the pharmaceutical order sheets. But the small machine wasn't working. She would have to go into town. She walked outside and unloaded the jeep, bringing the pies and other stuff into the kitchen and leaving them all on the table for Mrs. Tunney to sort out.

Then she drove into town, photocopied the sheets, and left the copies at the police station for Allie Voegler. They wouldn't really be that helpful because a lot of the drugs she had ordered which appeared on the sheets had already been dispensed on her rounds. No, she couldn't reconstruct what drugs she had dispensed from memory. She would have had to consult her files, and the thief had strewn them all over the floor.

She spent the next few hours shopping in town, buying things she really didn't need, trying not to think. She bought boots and stationery and three jars of sweet red peppers. She bought five magazines, including *Vogue*, a mystery novel, and a travel guide to the Sonora Desert and its environs.

Then she went home, climbed slowly to her room, and, without eating supper, fell into a deep and troublesome sleep, fully clothed.

When she awoke, clammy and hot, she was startled at the time. She had slept straight through the night. It was ten minutes after five in the morning. She hurriedly undressed and showered, then dressed for the day.

Dawn was slowly breaking. She was about to head downstairs to make coffee when she saw through the north side window what appeared to be a figure walking on the grounds.

Didi peered out. There definitely was someone, but it wasn't light enough to make out particulars.

Who was wandering about her property at this hour? Then she realized that the figure had probably come from the house . . . from the back entrance.

Didi watched, fascinated, a bit frightened. The figure walked slowly toward the pine forest. Beams of light were rapidly penetrating the darkness. By the time the mysterious figure reached the pine forest, Didi knew who it was:

Abigail. And she was carrying a small bag of some sort.

The moment Abigail vanished into the forest, Didi went downstairs quickly. The sighting of the figure had made her feel that she was watching something evil unfold. It was obvious that the events of the previous day still agitated her. She could not shake the logic that she was now among enemies.

She sat at the long table until the coffee was brewed.

Mrs. Tunney came in at six. She was startled to see Didi there and the coffee ready. "No exercise this morning, miss?" she asked.

"No," Didi replied and said no more.

Five minutes later, Charlie entered, still grumpy from sleep.

"Could I speak to you outside for a minute, Charlie?" she asked, but it came out as an order.

Didi walked out. And Charlie followed.

The moment Charlie Gravis closed the door she said: "I saw Abigail going into the pine forest about five-thirty this morning, Charlie. Can you tell me what that's all about?"

Charlie rubbed his grizzled eyes and laughed. "Oh, Miss Quinn, it's just Abigail going for her walk. She goes there about three mornings a week. No one knows why. Maybe *she* doesn't even know why. Your mother once told me, may she rest in peace, that she believes Abigail has built a little chapel in the forest. And she goes there to pray."

Didi stared hard at him. She didn't believe him. Just like she didn't believe that crazy story Mrs. Tunney told her about Dick Obey poaching mourning doves.

Charlie picked up on her skepticism.

"Believe me, Miss Quinn, that's all there is to it." Then he added: "Trent and I will clean up the clinic this morning."

"You do that," Didi said angrily. Charlie walked back into the house.

Didi walked into the space where she usually did her yoga exercises but she did not assume the lotus position. She had too much on her mind. And the first order of business, she knew, was to find out exactly what Abigail did in the pine forest. And why. Now, she knew, there were no innocents in her mother's house.

Chapter Fifteen

The alarm rang at four-thirty in the morning. Didi reached out with one hand and shut it off. She had laid her clothes out at the end of the bed before she went to sleep so that she would be able to dress quickly. A minute after she awoke she was standing at the window, fully dressed, vigilant, waiting for Abigail.

She had waited the previous morning in vain. But it would be this morning if Charlie was right and she went into the pine forest three times a week. As she stood there and as the day slowly began to form, she felt both silly and treacherous. It was no way to greet the dawn.

Then she saw Abigail. The young woman was once again heading toward the pine forest, a small package in her hand.

Didi walked quickly and silently down the stairs and out the front door. By the time Abigail entered the tree line, Didi was only thirty yards behind her.

But the moment Didi stepped onto the soft

carpet of pine needles and cones that covered the forest floor, she felt her old fear of the forest, inculcated by imaginative children's books replete with witches and goblins.

By the time Didi had recovered her adult perspective on pine forests, Abigail had vanished. But Didi had a sense of the direction the young woman had taken and she followed that vector.

From the rising sun, which began to flood the high trees with tastes of light, she could tell she was walking northeast, toward the oldest white pines. The forest was silent except for the manic triphammers of the woodpeckers.

Didi broke into a trot but the soft thickness of the forest floor sucked her feet in, and the trot tired her quickly.

Then she found Abigail's trail in the carpetlike forest floor.

She had been following the clearly visible tracks for not more than five minutes when she heard the screech.

It was such a strange sound. It was so jarring. Didi had simply never heard such an animal sound before. And it had to be an animal sound, she thought.

She heard it three times and the last time it sounded more like a scream. The source of the sound had to be very close.

Didi pressed on and came upon Abigail so suddenly that she had to drop to the ground instantly so that her presence was not noted by the golden-haired girl.

She had stumbled onto a very strange place and a very strange scene.

It was a small clearing. Abigail was standing in front of what appeared to be a very high open shed, covered on all sides by strong mesh wire.

Inside the shed was the creature that had produced the screech.

It was a falcon; for the most part white, with some yellow and black markings about the face and wings.

From where Didi lay, absolutely still, she could see Abigail reach into her bag, remove some pieces of raw meat, and begin to feed the falcon through the mesh. The young woman laughed as the falcon took the meat with a snap of its beak and neck. It was obvious that her affection for the creature was great.

As Didi lay there, unobserved, not more than twenty yards from an ecstatic Abigail, the ground dew began to seep into her clothes. But the growing physical discomfort meant little to her. She was caught up in this totally unexpected scenario. She remembered her mother's words, as recounted by Charlie Gravis . . . that Abigail had some kind of secret chapel in the woods . . . that she went there to pray. There was truth to those words, she realized. Abigail's feeding of the raptor with a kind of awed joy might be construed as prayer . . . as some kind of religious experience.

Didi began to feel extremely uneasy at her spying. It was like interfering with a secret communion.

But the bird itself fascinated her. She studied it as the falcon ravenously snatched the raw meat from Abigail's hand through the mesh.

It was an uncommon bird. It had the size and shape of the magnificent peregrine falcon. But it had the white color of its larger northern cousin—the gyrfalcon. The fact of the matter was, if Didi had seen this falcon in the wild, there would be no way she could identify it at all.

Suddenly there was another sound in the pine forest. Didi tensed and pressed herself tighter against the dewy ground.

A young man entered the clearing.

It was Trevor Brice.

Abigail laughed, a lovely laugh, and ran to him.

They embraced passionately, almost wildly. Then Trevor picked Abigail off her feet and swung her around in his arms. Didi was dazed. First of all, it had never dawned on Didi that a shy young woman like Abigail would have a lover. And if she did have a lover somewhere in the Hillsbrook area, "bad boy" Trevor Brice would be Didi's last guess. After all, he was the one she had accused of being the trigger man for George Hammond.

Didi wanted to leave. But she knew that if she moved now she would be discovered.

The two young people sunk to their knees together on the pine carpet and began to make love.

Didi closed her eyes. A wave of shame came over her. She felt she was a voyeur. She felt that she was somehow defiling the beauty and passion of the scene.

Oh! How embarrassing and pathetic this adventure had turned out to be! Why had she followed Abigail anyway?

Had she really believed that it was Abigail who had stolen the photos from the bird cage and faked the robbery? No.

Had she really believed that Abigail was implicated in the murder of Dick Obey? Of course not.

She kept her eyes closed but the sounds of lovemaking washed over her. She was only a few years older than Abigail but she felt, lying there, that they were separated by centuries.

Why hadn't she been able to accept the reality of her failure? Allie Voegler was right. Hammond and Trevor did not murder Dick Obey. Why was she resurrecting the whole mess again, just because her office had been trashed and the envelope was missing from the parrot cage?

What if she had not put the photos in the parrot cage?

What if she had forgotten and hid them somewhere else?

She wanted to press her hands against her ears but she was afraid to move.

I have to end this obsession with the corpse of Dick Obey, she thought. *I have to start concentrating again on veterinary work.* And there was a lot of it for her to do. In another week she was scheduled to start visiting Avignon Farms a few times a week while Dr. Hull was up in Saratoga. And she had to judge several classes at the Dutchess County Fair that was opening in ten days in Rhinebeck.

And she had to chair another meeting of the rabies committee. Even though George Hammond had been suspended, he had selected Howard Danto, the amorous goat farmer, to fill Dick Obey's chair on the committee, and there had to be a meeting soon. Yes, there was much to do. She was Doctor Nightingale. Not Sherlock Nightingale.

And then the last desperate cries of love pierced the white pine forest.

Silence. Didi opened her eyes. Abigail and Trevor lay in each other's arms, exhausted. The white falcon preened in the shed.

Now, she thought. Now is the time to escape unnoticed. Slowly, carefully, she began to inch away from that strange clearing. When she was about fifty yards away she rose and took long, resolute, carefully placed strides. Then she broke into a run.

By the time she left the tree line she was exhausted and dropped to one knee.

She could see Charlie Gravis standing calmly at the back of the house, as if he were waiting for her.

Didi waved. He waved back. Yes, she thought, it is time to go on rounds.

Chapter Sixteen

Didi drove into Rhinebeck alone on the first day of the Dutchess County Fair.

She was a bit nervous because it had been so long since she had attended one of these fairs—she could not remember how the judges dressed.

She had decided on a rather severe pair of riding breeches, a riding jacket, a shirt with a Peter Pan collar, and a pair of rain boots. All she could do was hope that was appropriate. She knew that she needed rain boots because summer storms were a given at the fair, particularly in the afternoons.

It was eight-thirty in the morning when she parked the jeep in the allotted judge's parking section. She made sure the identification tag was properly placed against the inside of the window so the jeep wouldn't be towed. Then she ambled toward the fair grounds. She had time to kill. Her first class to judge was heifers at ten o'clock. Then yearling bulls at one.

Physically, the fair was exactly the same as it had been when she was a child. A long fairway with all kinds of gaming booths on either side. Then dozens of small tents with food and drink and knickknacks of all kinds for sale. Past these were the large tents with indoor rings. Alongside the tents were pens with split rail fences for the sheep judging.

It was hot already and there was dust. The morning sun was like a red medallion.

She peered into each of the gaming booths. There were rings and basketball hoops and the eternal airgun targets—ducks paddling in a line. There were balloons to be pierced with darts. And milk bottles to be knocked over by baseballs. The prizes for winning these events had not changed either—hats or teddy bears or stuffed snakes or drinking glasses.

Several hands were beginning to set up on either side of the fairway. Hawkers were already out selling programs and banners and buttons and sun hats.

In the distance, away from the morning sun, she could see the trailers of those who had brought their animals from the far reaches of the county to participate in the judging events. And the Dutchess County Fair was big . . . all inclusive . . . there were events for ponies, horses, ducks, chickens, vegetables, pies, cookies, cows, sheep, goats . . . for everything under the sun that is grown or reared or made. For

163

all, there was a blue ribbon or a red ribbon or a white ribbon or a purple ribbon. It was a riot of democratic meritocracy. No matter your station in life or how you dressed or spoke—the lettuce you grew would be judged only by its lettuceness. And the lamb you raised would be judged only by its conformation. And the dog you trained would be judged only by its abilities.

Didi began to feel good, relaxed. She walked to one of the tents and ordered a container of coffee and a home-baked cinnamon donut. Both were delicious. She finished the donut quickly and just stood at the end of the fairway, sipping the coffee and watching the families with eager children enter the fairground.

When she finished the coffee she realized it was time to check in at the judge's tent. She turned and walked toward the administrative tents, which were identified by red, white, and blue banners flying above them.

"Didi! Didi Nightingale!"

Didi stopped and turned back toward the fairway when she heard her name being called.

She saw a woman down the fairway waving at her and calling her name. She couldn't make out who it was.

Didi waved back and waited.

The woman was walking swiftly towards her. Didi noticed her red hair but still couldn't make out her features.

Then she realized who it was. Emily Matthiessen. That woman from Kent, Connecticut, who had told her that Dick Obey had been murdered . . . who had been Dick Obey's lover . . . who had vanished from her gate house.

Didi, confused at seeing her again, took a tentative step toward the approaching woman.

Then the woman stopped abruptly.

And the moment she stopped walking, or perhaps a moment before or a moment after—an ugly sound cracked through the morning air. It was a gunshot.

Emily Matthiessen began to waver, to move back and forth as if she were a performer about to launch into a song.

Didi saw the blood spreading across Emily's face.

She ran to the woman.

Emily Matthiessen fell into Didi's outstretched arms. But Didi couldn't hold the weight and the woman's body slipped through and onto the ground.

She was dead. The bullet had entered the center of her forehead. The front of Didi's jacket was striped with blood.

Didi sat calmly on a small canvas cot in the fair's infirmary tent. The Rhinebeck police had just left. Didi had told them what she knew about the woman, although she had left out virtually everything concerning Dick Obey, other than that they had been lovers and both of them were now dead.

It was past noon already and it was obvious that Didi would miss all her judging assignments this day. She knew where she was. She could speak and listen correctly. But she was in a state of shock. Everything was disembodied . . . too calm.

A nurse appeared in a ludicrously starched white outfit and handed her a cup of tea. Didi sipped it.

The nurse said: "Why don't you just lay down for a while."

Didi didn't argue. She drank some more tea, handed the cup back to the nurse, and lay down on the cot, kicking off her rain boots. She fell fast asleep.

When she awoke she had a bad headache and there was a man seated at the end of the cot.

Didi, startled, swung her legs over the side. Then she realized it was Allie Voegler.

"I'm not here in an official capacity," he said. "It's not my jurisdiction. I'm here as a friend."

She nodded. He asked: "Was that the Connecticut woman?" She nodded in affirmation. And then, for the first time since the horrible shooting, she burst into tears and sobbed. Allie Voegler stared down at his shoes.

She fought back her tears and tried to stand but her legs were wobbly. She sat back down.

"You know," she said, half to Allie and half to herself: "You can't be a veterinarian if you're squeamish about blood or violent death. You simply can't. And I'm not. It wasn't that. It was when she fell into my arms . . . I had this feeling . . . this certainty . . . that it was somehow I who killed her. That the murderers were just waiting for her to contact me again. That sooner or later I would lead them to her . . . I would inadvertently set her up to die."

Allie Voegler replied gently: "I think you may be right. The Rhinebeck police found the shell casing. The shooter was parked near your jeep in the lot. He might well have followed you here. It seems that he used a high-powered hunting rifle with a scope. He must have calmly sighted the weapon from over the hood. Right out in the open."

"And no one saw anything?" she asked.

"No witnesses at all," Allie affirmed.

Then he pulled out a small notepad and flipped the pages. "But I do have some information you may find interesting. Off the record, you know. This isn't my jurisdiction . . . and it sure as hell ain't yours."

He flipped the pages again. "First of all, Matthiessen was a phony name. Her real name was Ceil Mann. She was at one time an assistant professor of environmental sciences at the State University in Oneonta. She left that and became director of the Raptor Research Center in Columbia County. It's a place where they get federal and state funds to rear all kinds of falcons and then release them into the wild. She left that job about a year ago and hasn't been heard of since."

"Damn!" Didi shouted, then picked up the pillow and flung it with all her might across the tent.

"What the hell is the matter with you?" Allie Voegler asked incredulously.

Didi buried her face in her hands. Allie Voegler's report had broken the floodgates.

For the first time she could at least begin to understand those perplexing little facts and events that had just slipped away in the past . . . that had really meant nothing to her.

She remembered the wounds on the wrist of Dick Obey which were definitely not made by dogs.

She remembered the tiny silver bells and the leather straps she had found in the abandoned gate house in Kent, Connecticut.

She remembered the story about Dick Obey poaching mourning doves.

And she remembered so clearly the chapel in the pine forest, with Abigail feeding the lovely white falcon in the wire mesh shed.

And she remembered the sounds of lovemaking between Abigail and Trevor Brice on the soft white pine carpet.

Trevor Brice. Always Trevor Brice. Always

there. On Dick Obey's property the night of the fire. In the pine forest week after week to meet his true love. Yes. But who was his true love? Abigail or the falcon?

Didi stood up suddenly, straight up. She breathed in and out. She turned to Allie Voegler, who was still sitting.

"You know Trevor Brice better than most people. You arrested him. Tell me how he makes a living."

A confused Allie Voegler asked: "What does that kid have to do with the woman who was murdered today?"

"Everything," Didi replied.

Allie shrugged. "Okay. He doesn't really make a living. From what I know he sponges off his father and he works three mornings a week, at the most."

"Doing what?"

"Well, it's not really steady work. But he drives for Frank Draper. He delivers to the New York restaurants for him."

Didi repeated the name, Frank Draper, Dick Obey's very best friend, as if she had never heard it before. Then she said to Allie: "I need your help again."

"For what?"

"I want to see where Trevor Brice goes . . . where he really goes on those delivery trips."

"He goes to restaurants in Manhattan."

Didi sat back down on the cot, very close to

Allie. She took his hand in hers. "Listen to me, Allie Voegler. We haven't been getting along. Let's bury the hatchet. Because if we don't the killing won't stop. It won't stop unless we stop it. Do you understand? And we can't stop it unless we're friends. Unless there's trust. Unless we can work together."

He stared for the longest time at their joined hands. Then he said: "I'll help you all I can just short of losing my job. I'm too lazy to try dairy farming."

She smiled. "Thank you."

Chapter Seventeen

Allie Voegler drove the jeep. It was not yet dawn when the spanking new pickup truck driven by Trevor Brice pulled off the Frank Draper farm, its bed loaded with crates of exotic vegetables. The red jeep followed discreetly, with lights dimmed, until the truck crossed the Hudson and headed south on the New York Thruway.

"Are you okay?" Allie Voegler asked her when they finally got onto the thruway. It was the first words either of them had spoken that morning.

"Yes, I'm fine."

"You look tense," he noted.

"I am tense. But I also feel fine."

Trevor Brice drove at high speed in the center lane, shuttling in and out to pass slower traffic. The red jeep kept falling behind and Allie Voegler had to accelerate into the fast lane from time to time in order to keep the pickup truck under surveillance.

"If he gets stopped by a State Trooper for speeding, it's meaningless," he said, "but if we get stopped, we lose him."

They didn't get stopped. And they didn't lose him, even after he turned off the thruway and wound his way to the George Washington Bridge. But once he crossed the bridge into Manhattan and headed downtown on Broadway, it was touch and go. They lost him three times between 166th and 103rd streets.

He made his first stop in the Lincoln Center area, at a small French restaurant on a side street. Then a restaurant in the theater district. Then four restaurants in the West Village and one in Tribeca.

At around eleven in the morning a light rain began to fall. Didi had to roll up the top of the jeep.

Trevor Brice stopped for lunch at a pushcart on Canal Street. He ordered two frankfurters and a can of soda. Then he began to work his way up the east side of Manhattan. Between Canal and East 79th streets he delivered organic vegetables to at least eight restaurants.

The two occupants of the red jeep silently and doggedly kept up their surveillance, fortified by numerous containers of coffee, assorted Danish and sandwiches, and an occasional tangerine. The tedium of the surveillance was obviously less for Allie than it was for Didi. She had been to the big city innumerable times. But

Allie Voegler hadn't been in Manhattan in years, since he was a boy, and he watched the proceedings wide-eyed. Just a country boy, Didi thought.

By four o'clock in the afternoon, it was obvious that this surveillance would not be fruitful. "Well," Allie said, "the kid earns his pay, that's for sure."

The pickup truck was empty of vegetables. Trevor Brice headed back downtown.

"Where is he going now?" Allie asked.

Then it became obvious that he was going to get out of Manhattan via the Lincoln Tunnel rather than the George Washington Bridge.

"Six of one, half a dozen of another," Didi said wearily. She was exhausted and angry and depressed.

"Well, we might as well follow him home," Allie said.

"We might as well."

The tunnel was backed up. It took forty minutes to crawl to the Jersey side.

Didi sank disconsolately into her seat. It had become oppressively hot in the vehicle but she just didn't have the strength to undo the top. The surveillance had been a disaster. Maybe next time. But how many times did they have? She was so close . . . and so far.

"Look at that fool!" Allie suddenly shouted.

Didi sat up straight. "What's the matter?"

"He took the wrong turn. He's going south on the Jersey Turnpike."

Allie slowed down. "He probably hustled drinks in those last few restaurants and now he doesn't know where the hell he's going. No reason we should be fools also. Let's go home."

"No," Didi said, "follow him." Allie shrugged and swung the jeep onto the approach road to the turnpike heading south.

It could be a drunken mistake, Didi thought, or it could be important. They had no choice but to follow. With the woman dead, she was sure that only Trevor Brice could lead them to . . . to whom? Frank Draper?

The pickup truck exited at the turnoff for Newark Airport but didn't enter the airport. Instead, Trevor led them onto a series of bypass roads. The terrain kept getting more desolate: swamps on both sides of the road, the view obscured by high cattails. The odor was intense and foul.

Then, suddenly, like a bad dream, ships loomed up on either side of them. Enormous ships straddled by even larger cranes that looked like bloodsucking dragonflies.

They realized they were in Port Newark.

Most of the vessels were container ships, their decks stacked with giant metal boxes.

The pickup parked about a hundred feet from a freighter. The name of the ship was *Bolivar Seven*.

They watched Trevor Brice leisurely leave his truck and saunter up to the loading dock. He started to speak to one of the seamen on the dock. They both lit cigarettes.

"Well, he sure isn't delivering vegetables now," Allie Voegler said.

The conversation lasted eighteen minutes. It became animated for a few moments but then ended calmly. The two men shook hands. Trevor Brice went back to his truck.

"What do we do now?" Allie asked.

"Let him go. Don't follow."

They both ducked down as the pickup wheeled past them, back toward the turnpike.

"Now what?" Allie pressed.

Didi hunched forward. Her eyes were on the freighter. "Find out what kind of ship that is. Where it's going."

"I'll do my best," Allie said.

He left the jeep and walked over to the loading platform. Didi watched him speak to one man very briefly, then another, who pointed to a third. This man seemed to be responding to his inquiry.

Allie walked purposefully back to the jeep and stood on the passenger side, next to her. "It's a Panamanian registry," he said. "But you'll never guess who leases it."

"Someone in Kuwait or Bahrein or maybe Qatar," she said softly.

His eyes widened. "How the hell did you

175

know that? You're right, Didi. A company from Bahrein. That's one of those oil sheikdoms, isn't it?"

"Get in," Didi said urgently. "We have to get back to Hillsbrook. I have to show you something."

It was dark when they arrived back in Hillsbrook. Didi instructed Allie Voegler to park the jeep some distance from her house, just off the road.

Then, flashlight in hand, she led him into the pine forest.

There was no need, however, to use the torch. The moon was full and bright. All they could hear as they walked was the sound of their own feet on the pine needle carpet and the occasional unidentified *whoosh* off in the distance. An owl hunting? A creature burrowing?

Didi found the clearing and the shed quickly, as if she had visited it dozens of times, instead of only once.

The falcon became excited when he saw them, expecting food.

Allie kept his distance. "What is it?" was his wary question.

"I would guess a hybrid. Half peregrine, half gyrfalcon. And it was probably hatched in what used to be Ceil Mann's research center."

"What is it doing here?"

"Being fed and cared for, and no doubt trained."

"Trained? For what?"

"For a falconer in the Middle East, perhaps Bahrein," Didi said.

Allie moved closer to the mesh. Didi continued: "For an oil rich sheik who would probably pay one hundred thousand dollars for a bird like this."

"Are you serious?"

"Quite serious, Allie. In America, falconry is a kind of romantic sport, indulged in by secretive, clubby eccentrics. But in the desert, it's a way of life. They will pay anything, even if they studied at Oxford."

Allie threw up his arms in exasperation. "Didi . . . is what you're telling me . . . that all this killing is about stolen falcons?"

"Stolen falcon chicks, probably. And then they're reared in sheds. Mrs. Tunney told me that my mother caught Dick Obey trapping mourning doves in this pine forest. Probably to feed the growing chicks."

"But, Didi. . . ."

"No, listen! Do you remember those leather straps and small bells I found in Kent? Now I know what they are. It was a matter of context. They meant nothing to me at the time. But the leather straps are jesses. They're used to tether the falcon to a fist or perch. And the bells are used to find the falcons if they get away when flying to a lure during training. You can hear the bells in the woods."

Allie objected. "You can't really train falcons around here. Too many people. And not enough flat open ground."

Didi ignored the objection. "And do you remember those strange marks on Dick Obey's corpse . . . on the hand? It's quite possible they were inflicted by a falcon during training. The bird lands on your hand with great force and the talons grasp and dig."

Allie did not protest anymore. He studied the bird.

"We're talking about millions of dollars," Didi declared, "if this has been going on for a few years and all their customers are from the Gulf States."

Allie shook his head stubbornly. "It doesn't make sense. If Dick Obey was involved, and all this money was being made, why did he get into that harebrained real estate scam with George Hammond?"

"Maybe he thought the falcon business was just too dangerous for him and his girlfriend, who had to be the source of the chicks. Maybe he was frightened . . . just plain frightened because the man he took orders from was violent. Maybe he just began to loathe this kind of larceny and felt safer in an old-fashioned real estate scam. I don't know. But I do know that, as sure as we're standing in a pine forest, Dick

Obey and his woman friend were murdered by the same person and, ultimately, for the same reason. They both wanted out."

"And you think Frank Draper is that person? You think his money comes from birds like these, not from organic farming?"

"I think so. But I'm also suspicious of John Theobold."

"Are you serious?"

"I think his wife and Dick Obey had an affair. And it may, as they say, have been business related. The business of falcons."

Didi paused. She twisted slowly from side to side. Her back was beginning to ache. She had been too long in the jeep that day following Trevor Brice.

Then she said: "The problem is . . . and it is a difficult problem . . . Which of our suspects has the sophistication to set up such an operation? After all, it involved contacting desert sheiks ten thousand miles away."

She shivered in the summer night. Suddenly the white pines had become threatening. They were talking theory. But they were both there, in the forest, in front of the falcon shed, because of two brutal murders.

"And Trevor Brice?" Allie asked.

"I think he does what anyone asks him to do, as long as you give him a drink and a twenty-dollar bill."

"But did he pull the trigger on Ceil Mann?"

"I don't know."

Didi sat down suddenly on the forest floor, assuming the lotus position, as if she were about to do her breathing exercises. But she did no yoga.

She stared at the magnificent bird of prey glaring at them through the mesh. Then she looked up at the equally dazzling moon.

"But it's all speculation, Didi," said Allie. "At best we can trace this falcon back to Ceil Mann's research center. Or arrest the man on the Panamanian vessel who is smuggling the birds into Bahrein. But murder? No. We have nothing."

Didi rolled the flashlight gently along the ground, back and forth, as though it was a child's toy. All during the trip home, she had been secretly wrestling with an ethical problem. Was it permissible to put an innocent person at risk in order to bring a killer to justice?

Now it was beginning to dawn on her that she had no other choice. She would simply have to depend on Allie Voegler to make sure the innocent were protected.

"I think I can flush the killer out," she said softly.

"What?"

"I can flush the killer out!"

"How?"

Didi patted the ground. Allie sat down next

to her, but not in the lotus position. She felt, for the first time, very close to him.

"Like the falconer brings the falcon back to his fist. When he lets the falcon fly free for the first time, he uses a lure. He swings a brightly colored object, usually studded with feathers and raw meat, to catch the falcon's eye. And the falcon returns to the lure even though he could just as well fly away to freedom."

Allie did not respond to her imagery.

"All we need is that scarecrow Charlie Gravis keeps by the side of the house. The one with the hat that he used to use when he had a field in alfalfa."

"Is that the lure?" Allie asked skeptically.

"No, Allie. The scarecrow is just a prop. I'm the lure. Me, and a young man in Delaware County named Jonah."

Then she told him her plan in detail. She spun it out of her hurt . . . out of her passion to end this mess of death. She laid it out with precision . . . as if she were planning a vaccination program.

When she was finished, he clambered to his feet and shouted at her: "I won't do that, Didi! It's dangerous. And it's kind of crazy."

She got up and walked over to him. She placed her hand gently on his cheek. His face was warm.

"We have no other option, Allie. Except to walk away."

Suddenly he pulled her hand away from his face. Then he threw her hand down. He walked to the falcon shed and ran his fingers along the mesh, angrily. The falcon mantled as if about to attack.

He turned back to her. His face was gentle now. In the moonlight, he seemed like a high school boy again.

"Why do I always have the feeling that I'm one of your patients . . . that I'm waiting in a stall for you to prescribe some loathsome medicine for me?"

Then he laughed at his own words and added: "You can count on me, Dr. Nightingale."

Chapter Eighteen

Didi walked into the back room of the Hillsbrook Diner at eight o'clock sharp on that dull, hot summer morning.

The entire rabies committee was already present: Frank Draper, Roger Brice, John Theobold, all waiting for Madam Chairman. And there was the newest member: Howard Danto.

It was immediately obvious to Didi that the old-timers on the committee had welcomed the gentleman goat farmer with open arms. There was no tension in the room.

Didi also noticed that the usual printout reporting new incidents of rabies in Dutchess and surrounding counties was absent from its usual place of honor—the center of the table. Then she realized that, with George Hammond suspended because of the land scam, there would be no printout available until a replacement was appointed. And that could be a long, long time.

Her entrance sent the assembled into a state of silent shock.

They had never seen Didi dressed like *this*!

She was wearing a tight-fitting low-cut light blue dress; high-heel shoes; lipstick and a flash of rouge. She held a large straw hat in her hand.

What they saw was so different from the usual nitty-gritty veterinary practitioner they frequently saw on the roads of Hillsbrook—all they could do at first was stare.

Didi smiled sweetly and sat down in her usual seat, extracting a pad and pencil from her purse.

Then Frank Draper said: "Damn, honey, you're a knockout."

And John Theobold looked away and seemed to blush.

Roger Brice said: "I think you finally got yourself a man. That's what I think."

And Howard Danto just grinned at her lasciviously.

Frank Draper then picked up on Roger Brice's theme: "Is that it, Didi? You got yourself a beau?"

Didi smiled. "Well," she asked them in a flirtatious tone, "wouldn't you say it's about time?"

They all applauded vigorously and banged their spoons on their coffee cups.

"Who the hell is it?" Frank Draper demanded.

Didi said: "He's not from around here. He's

from Delaware County, the other side of Delhi."

"At least he's a dairy farmer, I hope," John Theobold mumbled.

"I'm sorry. No. In fact, he's a motel clerk."

"That solves a lot of problems," Howard Danto observed humorously.

"But isn't it a bit early to get a room? Damn. It's only eight o'clock in the morning," Frank Draper noted lewdly.

"I won't be seeing him until tonight," Didi explained. "But I'm taking the day off after this meeting. I'm going on a shopping spree at the Hudson Mall. And then I'm going to meet some old school friends for lunch in Kingston."

She opened her pad and tapped her pencil on the table, signaling that it was time to end the small talk and commence the meeting.

But Roger Brice said: "Didi, how can you expect us to concentrate on rabies when you look like that?"

"Let's try," she said sweetly.

She started to describe the new program to them. How state workers are laying out thousands of vaccine-laced pieces of bait for raccoons, which will enable them to develop rabies antibodies.

Their minds slowly drifted away from her newfound allure. When Didi dropped that dreadful statistic—more than 1,000 treated cases of rabies in humans in 1992 as against only 90 in 1986—they started to pay close attention.

Didi followed the scenario even though, for the most part, it was meaningless. She went to the Hudson Mall and shopped. Then she went to Kingston and had lunch. Alone, not with friends.

At one o'clock she parked her red jeep in a garage, walked across the street and rented a car. The jeep was simply too noticeable. Then she headed west on Route 28 toward the Sunshine Motel.

At the first gas station she came to, she went into the bathroom and changed out of her seductive outfit into work clothes.

It was a painful ride for Didi. Not only did she dislike the rented car . . . not only was she frightened that the plan might not work and expose her to Allie Voegler for the bumbling amateur she was—but the dead seemed to be materializing in the passenger seat.

No matter how loud she played the radio, she kept having the feeling that Dick Obey was momentarily beside her, and then that woman he probably loved, Ceil Mann. And then, of all people, her mother, clucking with disapproval about something or other, but then smiling her radiant smile that always meant everything would be fine.

Heat stroke, she thought. Tension and heat

stroke. So she rolled up all the windows to keep the choking summer air out, and put on the air conditioner full tilt until the inside of the car was frigid.

Finally, frozen and tense, she reached the Sunshine Motel.

It was just past 3:30 P.M. She parked off the road as if she had just stopped for a rest and to gaze down at the lovely meadow on the far side of the motel structure.

She turned off the radio and the air conditioner and opened all the windows. Late afternoon bumblebees were working outside the car. She could hear their buzzing in the wildflowers.

From where she had parked she could see through the window of the motel office where Jonah worked. The slim figure with the baseball hat was clearly visible because the afternoon sun was behind her. She also had a clear view of the eight cars on the motel parking lot.

Didi waited. Her hands held the steering wheel and became progressively tighter as the wait lengthened.

The heat was oppressive. A hundred things could go wrong. Everything depended on Allie Voegler. Everything. What if he had decided not to go through with it at the last moment and wasn't able to reach her? What if he had simply gotten cold feet or once and for all decided that she was irrational? What if he had been involved in an accident on the way to Delaware County and was now unconscious in some emergency room somewhere?

And, worst of all, what if the "lure" did not bring the "falcon"?

A bead of sweat rolled down her forehead and temporarily blinded her in one eye.

She heard the bumblebees again. They seemed to be working right under the car and up along the doors. The sound of the bees for some reason brought back the sound of love-making she had heard in the forest. Didi winced. A sudden stab of memory. Didi Night-ingale and Drew Pelletier making love with the same desperate need and abandon as Trevor Brice and Abigail. Not in a pine forest, though. In a motel on the Delaware River.

The sweat was in her palms now. It was the abandon of love she missed most. The ability to forget . . . to let go . . . to not give a damn. She wiped the sweat from her palms along the sides of her jeans and grasped the steering wheel again.

Then she heard the shot.

And the window of the motel office exploded.

Didi ran out of the car and down the slope toward the motel, scrambling and tripping on the overgrown incline.

She saw Allie Voegler run from one of the motel rooms, holding his gun by his side.

"Stay back, Didi!" he shouted.

She saw where he was headed. A Plymouth

minivan parked the wrong way in the rear of the lot. The back window was pulled open.

Allie Voegler reached the van and crouched. "I'm a police officer," he shouted. "Throw the rifle out! Throw it out now!"

Didi stopped ten feet from the van. She was trembling. She couldn't catch her breath. She smelled a strange smell—cheese.

The rifle fell out of the window. Allie darted in and kicked it away from the van.

Then he shouted: "Get out of the vehicle! Keep your hands over your head. Get out! Get out!"

The door opened. A large man climbed out carefully, trying to keep his hands over his head without losing his balance.

Allie Voegler kicked the man's feet out from under him and he fell heavily. In seconds, he was cuffed.

Didi stared dumbly at the face and form of Howard Danto.

Then Jonah came out of the motel office, walking quickly toward the van, and dragging behind him a scarecrow whose head had been more or less blown apart by the rifle shot. Strangely enough, the baseball cap used to simulate the real Jonah was somehow still attached. He dropped the scarecrow beside Howard Danto. Jonah was pale.

Allie took very deep breaths and broke into a huge grin. "Didi, I did what you told me. But

I never really believed it would happen. I never believed he would show up. Damn! You are one helluva criminal investigator. The top of the line. I thought all that stuff you told me about luring the falcon was garbage."

Didi replied quietly. "I had no idea that Howard was the murderer. He never was a suspect in my mind. Now, it makes sense. Sudden money. Worldwide contacts. Now it makes sense.

"But I did know that the murderer of Dick Obey and Ceil Mann would have to kill Jonah if he believed I was sleeping with him. Because the murderer had to have been following me. That was the way he caught up to Ceil Mann—watching me, waiting for her to contact me again.

"So he also had to know that I had been out to the Sunshine Motel and Jonah had talked to me about Dick Obey. Maybe he didn't know how much Jonah knew. Maybe there are secrets hidden here that Jonah might know. He couldn't take the chance."

"You were bloody brilliant," Allie Voegler said.

Howard Danto sat up and stared straight ahead.

Allie shook his head. "Look at the gentleman farmer. Murderous son of a bitch! Well, with the rifle, we have him cold for the murder of Ceil Mann and the attempted murder of Jonah.

He'll never taste goat cheese again, much less make it. That's for sure."

Didi said: "I want him tried for the murder of Dick Obey, not the others."

"What the hell does it matter, Didi?"

She took a step towards Danto. Hatred for this man suddenly clawed at her.

"I want to hear from your own lips that you murdered Dick Obey." Her words were clipped, as if she had trouble with the language.

Danto was silent. His sweat-drenched body was like a broken whale's.

"Do you hear me?" she shouted. "I want to hear it from you."

He said nothing.

Did ran at him, her fists hitting him on the face and shoulder. He rolled away.

Allie grabbed her. "What are you doing? What the hell is the matter with you? The man is in handcuffs."

She broke away from his grip and stared across the lovely meadow. Yes, she had lost control, she realized. Yes, she was acting like a fool. She breathed in and out slowly, as if she were about to do yoga. The meadow was calming. The carpet of wildflowers was like a sedative. She kept her eyes on the meadow.

It would have been so nice, she thought, to walk with Dick Obey in such a meadow, arm in arm, talking about cows perhaps. About anything.

She blinked away tears. She felt Dick Obey's presence strongly. As if he were there, in the meadow.

Suddenly she felt cold. Very cold.

"Are you okay?" she heard Allie ask.

She looked at the meadow again. Did Dick Obey die in that meadow?

She wheeled. "Allie," she said, "do you remember what you said when I showed you that white falcon in the pine forest?"

"No."

"You said that it was hardly possible to train a falcon in Hillsbrook. Too many people and too many hills."

She gestured toward the meadow. "But you can train a falcon here, can't you, Allie? Tall trees surrounding a large flat meadow. Ideal, isn't it?"

She took a few steps back toward Howard Danto and pointed at him. "Tell me, Allie, why is he sweating so? Why is his three-hundred-dollar embroidered, hand-tailored denim shirt black with sweat?"

"Fear, I guess. And the heat. It's hot here, Didi."

"No, Allie. That's work sweat. Isn't that right, Mr. Danto? You've been working hard."

She headed toward the minivan and started to climb in.

"Stay out of there, Didi," Allie shouted.

She ignored him, grabbed the shovel lying on

the back seat and flung it out of the van along with a few rounds of goat cheese—Howard Danto's finest.

"You see, Allie, he was digging. That's what made him all sweaty. Digging in the meadow!"

Then, like a madwoman, she began to search the van, flinging objects out onto the ground, ignoring Allie's pleas.

When she finally emerged she was holding a small canvas satchel—triumphantly.

She dumped the contents on the ground between Allie Voegler and Howard Danto.

The objects were filthy, as if they had been covered with dirt.

There was a pair of large gloves. A strange, wooden, decoylike bird carving with bedraggled feathers stapled on. And a long leather line.

Didi crouched over them. She was beginning to feel ill.

She poked at the gloves. "Falconer's gloves," she explained to Allie.

Then she pointed at the decoy-type carving. "A lure to bring the falcon down."

Then she pointed to the line. "A leather line to swing the lure."

There was silence. "Don't you understand, Allie?" she asked, almost desperately.

"No," he admitted.

"Dick Obey was murdered in that meadow. While he was training a falcon. He probably told Danto that he wanted out. That Ceil Mann wanted out, too. So Howard Danto put the gloves on and used the lure line to strangle him. There probably was a struggle. But Danto is fifty pounds heavier and fifteen years younger. Then he dumped the body on the road at night, and smeared it with blood so that the dogs would mutilate it. Don't you see, Allie? He buried the gloves and the lure line in the meadow. But then he fell for *my* lure—that Jonah was my lover. He couldn't take a chance. He returned and dug up the murder weapon and tried to kill Jonah."

Didi buried her face in her hands for a moment. Then she looked up at the meadow and pointed. "Dick Obey was murdered right there. In that lovely place. Oh God, Allie, how sad!"

It was Jonah who took Didi by the arm and led her gently into a vacant motel room.

She lay down on the bed. He closed the shades, turned up the air conditioner, and left.

Didi felt as if the blood had been drained from her body. So much had happened . . . but for some reason, the moment Jonah had left her alone, the only thing she could think of was a goat . . . what Howard Danto's lovely French Alpine doe called Laura would do once her master was imprisoned. Who would weep for Laura?

It was past midnight when the red jeep returned to Hillsbrook. Didi had one more stop to make before she climbed into her bed. She had one more knot to untie.

Didi walked into the "servant's" quarters and knocked quietly on Charlie Gravis's door. This time Charlie was awake and dressed.

"Can't sleep, Charlie?" she asked.

"Someone stole the old scarecrow," Charlie complained. "And I dearly loved that old thing."

"I'm sure whoever took it," Didi said, "put it to good use." Then she asked: "Could you come into the kitchen with me for a minute, Charlie?" Charlie obediently followed her into the kitchen and they both sat down in the darkness at the long table.

"People called today, Miss Quinn. No one knew where you were. We were getting worried."

"I was in Delaware County."

Charlie did not respond to that fact.

Didi folded her hands on the table. This will be painful, she thought.

"My mother knew about the shed in the pine forest . . . didn't she, Charlie?"

"What shed?" he replied.

"And she knew about the falcons, didn't she, Charlie?"

"What falcons?"

"There's no reason to cover up anymore, Charlie. It's all over. Howard Danto has been arrested for murder. And Trevor Brice as an accomplice to murder. The whole thing is over.

No more falcons. No more sheds. No more mourning doves. It's over. Done with. So, I'm asking you again, Charlie."

"What is it you're asking me again, Miss Quinn?"

"Did my mother know about the shed? Did she know about the falcons?"

"Miss Quinn, you're tired. You ought to go to bed. There haven't been falcons in Hillsbrook for a long time. Just a few chicken hawks, riding the wind."

The old man stood up and walked back toward his room.

"Charlie!" she shouted after him. "Why won't you tell the truth to me? Why won't you talk to me?"

The old man stopped. "But I am talking to you, Miss Quinn. It's just that you can't hear. Things were very bad in Hillsbrook a few years ago. When you were in Philadelphia or India; I forget which. Do you know what I mean? Very bad. Farmers were losing their herds every day. Going broke. Going under. The milk truck didn't stop here anymore. And they couldn't even keep their busted farms to live on. Because the banks were there to swoop down. And the developers were waiting just behind the banks. We had seven suicides in two years, Miss Quinn.

"And you know the way dairy farmers do it. Always that stupid shotgun in the mouth. Ugly as hell. I have to go to sleep now, Miss Quinn. I'm an old man. Got to get my sleep."

And then he vanished down the corridor.

Didi's eyes caught the empty parrot cage swinging ever so gently from the kitchen ceiling.

Then she lay her face down on the table. She was so weary. Had her mother been some kind of rural Robin Hood? Allowing thieves and murderers access to her land in the belief that such an action would help the struggling dairy farmers? Would she ever know?

She looked back at the parrot cage, still swinging slowly in the dark kitchen. "Do parrots have souls, Mommy?" That was the question she had asked her mother when Hope and Charity arrived on the scene.

"I have no idea," her mother had replied. Then she had added: "And if they don't, they really don't need them. After all, they have wings."

Didi fell fast asleep at the long kitchen table, her face on her hands.

Her nap lasted only fifteen minutes.

She was abruptly wakened by a cold feeling against her face . . . like an ice cube.

Didi stared at the barrel of a shotgun, the muzzle of which was pressed against the right side of her face.

It was Charlie Gravis's shotgun . . . the one she had seen in his room.

But the person holding it was Abigail.

The pressure of the steel on her face was painful.

"Why are you doing this?" Didi whispered, the fear like a vise on her throat.

Abigail didn't answer. She was wearing an old black slip, much too large for her. Had it been Didi's mother's slip once? And no shoes or socks or slippers. Her hair was wild.

All Didi could see in her eyes was hate.

I am going to die, she thought. I am going to be shot to death in my mother's kitchen.

Then she saw the chain around Abigail's neck. Hanging from it was a small watch . . . inverted . . . so that the wearer could look down and see the time.

It was a lovely thing. Obviously an antique. Thin. Gold. Delicate. With a tiny, beautifully worked bird of prey coming out of either side near the top . . . like wings . . . like cherubim used to be carved on the sides of wall clocks.

What will be the time when I die? Didi asked herself.

Abigail pushed the shotgun even harder against Didi's face. Then she said bitterly: "You like this watch around my neck? He gave it to me. Trev. Because he loves me. And I love him. And now you have killed all of us."

There was such terrible anguish in Abigail's face and voice that Didi thought for a brief moment that she deserved to die. The thought allayed her fear somewhat. As if what was about to happen was just.

Didi could see Abigail's hand depress the trigger even more. Would it be painful? Would the first few slugs in the pattern kill her instantly? I want to live, Didi thought.

"Isn't it a bit early in the morning to be making coffee?"

The booming, complaining voice came from the corridor.

And then a bathrobed Mrs. Tunney came into the kitchen and flicked on the light.

She rubbed the sleep out of her eyes.

"It's one-thirty in the morning," she yelled.

Then she saw Abigail with the shotgun. "Aren't you a little too old to be playing with toys?" she asked Abigail and then slapped the gun aside. Abigail crouched on the floor and began to weep, wildly, desperately.

"Shouldn't you go upstairs now, miss?" Mrs. Tunney suggested to the shaken Didi. Then she helped her up and guided her toward the hallway.

As Didi started to climb the stairs to her mother's bedroom, she heard Mrs. Tunney call out to her: "The child don't mean no harm, miss. You know how it is out here in the country. People get lonely. People get crazy."

Yes, Didi thought, I know how it is.

DON'T MISS THE NEXT
BOOK IN THE
DR. NIGHTINGALE SERIES,
DR. NIGHTINGALE RIDES
THE ELEPHANT,
COMING TO YOU
FROM SIGNET IN
AUGUST 1994.

It was simply too cold that February morning to sit on the bare ground, so Didi placed a piece of cardboard down and then assumed the lotus position to begin her daily yogic breathing.

Her heart, however, wasn't in her exercises that morning. And it wasn't only because of the cold. She was going to the circus!

There would be no veterinary work today. No rounds. No clinic. No goats with sexual problems. No horses cast in their stall. No dogs with ticks. No cows with stringy milk.

Didi dearly loved being a veterinarian. But she loved the circus more. Even at twenty-eight she still had a child's enthusiasm for the Big Top.

She wasn't going to the Ringling Bros. and Barnum & Bailey Circus in Madison Square Garden, where her mother had taken her every year from the age of four on. No, this was a small one-ring traveling circus that was setting up on the grounds of what had once been Sennett College, on the outskirts of Hillsbrook—equidistant, in fact, from the three towns of Rhinebeck, Poughkeepsie, and Hillsbrook.

And the trip wasn't sheerly for pleasure. The circus people wanted to interview her for the job of veterinarian-in-residence during their twenty-day run. For Didi, a chance to be near Asian elephants again was a gift from the gods.

She grimaced when she realized that Sara, the Spotted Poland China Sow, was taking an intense interest in the breathing exercises. She was staring at Didi with those intense pig eyes from between the slate of the farrowing pen. According to the 114-day cycle, Sara was due to give birth in three days.

Didi had known the pig problem would eventually get out of hand. She should have stopped it when she first came back to Hillsbrook . . . when she came home to practice veterinary medicine in farm country, where she had grown up.

But Didi had come home to find herself heir to a quartet of "retainers"—Charlie Gravis, Mrs. Tunney, Trent Tucker, and Abigail. All her mother's loyal employees were now, crazily, for better or worse, under Didi's reluctant protection.

All four swore that the pigs were family pets who had been much loved by Didi's mother. Of course, they had lied. Every autumn the quartet slaughtered two of the hogs—the so-called family pets—no matter what Didi said. They ate most of the meat and sold the rest. And Didi had never dared to stop it, although she constantly complained. She really didn't mind their selling the meat—after all, they received no wages from her, only room and board in the big house. It was the slaughter she couldn't handle.

What with the cold and the staring sow and her thoughts of the circus, she did a very abbreviated breathing routine and then ran into the house. Mrs. Tunney was preparing her signature breakfast dish: oatmeal. Charlie Gravis, Didi's geriatric veterinary assistant, was seated at the table along with Abigail and young Trent Tucker. They were all bundled up against the chill.

Didi announced the schedule to them. "We'll leave about ten-thirty. The matinee starts at noon, and Mr. Allenbach has left tickets for all of us. I have to meet with him at about eleven-fifteen. We'll take the Jeep. It'll be a close fit, but we can all get in."

She waited for their joyous response. They huddled over their bowls, waiting for the magical oatmeal Mrs. Tunney was stirring in her enormous kettle. Even the ethereal, golden-haired Abigail looked grim. And Trent Tucker, who usually had a quip for every occasion, seemed to be contemplating the contours of his spoon.

Who can deal with these people? Didi thought, and strode angrily out of the kitchen, through the hallway, up the stairs, and into her mother's old bedroom. She flung herself down on the bed to brood.

They all left in Didi's red Jeep promptly at ten-thirty, a solid mass of parkas, scarves, fur-lined boots, and mittens.

Didi played Patsy Cline tapes all the way there. Abigail and Trent Tucker hummed along. Charlie Gravis pouted—he did not like Patsy. Mrs. Tunney seemed not to be hearing the music at all.

What an odd group we are, Didi thought. Dr. Didi Quinn Nightingale, DVM, and her four elves.

They arrived at the old Sennett College site at eleven o'clock sharp. A huge tent had been set up with a banner proclaiming the name of the circus, THE ORIGINAL DALTON'S BIG TOP CIRCUS, and the dates of the performances.

Behind the tent was the semicircle of mobile homes where the circus performers lived. And behind these were four large trailer trucks, one of which had cages on a flatbed. It was obvious that this small circus did not tour via Amtrak.

Didi went alone to the small mobile home that also functioned as an administrative office.

The manager, Thomas Allenbach, was seated on a large carton, eating a turkey sandwich and sipping from a bottle of soda. He was a young man in his early thirties, with longish sandy hair and a well-trimmed beard. He wore a muffler and a hiking vest.

"Can I help you?" he asked brightly.

"I'm Doctor Nightingale," she said.

He stared at her, wide-eyed. He didn't answer. She waited. Then he put his sandwich down.

"I'm sorry. I'm sorry. It's just that you surprised me. I never expected the vet I would be interviewing would be so pretty and so young."

"Well, I think you're pretty, too," Didi retorted, trying to nip this kind of nonsense in the bud. It worked. He got right to the point.

"You were recommended to us highly. It's a twenty-day run here, and we need someone to stop in at least once a day and check the animals out. And to be on call if anything happens."

"It's also state law," Didi reminded him.

"I'm aware of that," he said, smiling.

"Could you tell me who recommended me?" She was genuinely curious.

He grinned wider and said, "I don't reveal my sources." Then he added: "But they did tell me that Didi Nightingale knows elephants."

Didi felt uncomfortable. The unnamed source who recommended her must have known that after vet school she had spent a year in Madras with Mr. Mohandas Medawar, probably the most respected researcher in the world in the realm of Asian elephants. But the same source probably did not know that she really hadn't done any real clinical, hands-on work while there. Medawar was conducting an ambitious study under the auspices of the Fund for Animals. Teams were being sent all over Asia to locate, count, and describe the conditions of elephants still used for work. Didi had been assigned to the team that wandered through Laos, Cambodia, Thailand, and Vietnam. It had been exciting, often dangerous, and she had seen many elephants up close, but she had rarely treated one. In Southwest Asian logging camps the mahouts have their own medicines.

No, she couldn't claim to "know" Asian elephants. But should she admit that fact to Allenbach?

Allenbach interpreted her silence as modesty. He continued, "So here's what we got. Five Asian elephants. All females. Three Bengal tigers. Two female and one male. And the Shetland ponies. That's it. The animals are in excellent condition."

For the first time Didi noticed that the walls of the mobile home were lined with political campaign buttons of all kinds from all eras. She could make out Clinton and Gore, Reagan and

Bush, Mondale and Ferraro, FDR, Dewey, Will-kie, and a host of others.

"And the pay, Doctor Nightingale, is two-eighty a week," he said, picking up his sandwich once again.

"Are you serious?" Didi shot back, astonished at the ridiculously low figure. She had expected a sum closer to $2,800 a week. It was a lot of work and a lot of responsibility.

"I'm afraid that's all we can afford."

"Well, thank you for the interview and the free tickets, Mr. Allenbach. But count me out." She started to walk out of the trailer.

"Wait!" Allenbach put the remainder of his lunch down again. "Don't take the low offer as a personal insult. That's what we pay. If you expected more, you have no understanding of what circuses are about now. We don't make money anymore. Even the big ones. Understand, the circus world is for the fools . . . the romantics . . . or those who just love a very old and very beautiful way of life and way of performing.

"The only reason my company keeps on going is because when the Soviet Union collapsed, all the great circus performers in Eastern Europe—and that's where the great acrobats and jugglers and clowns always were—started to come to the U.S. They came in waves and they worked for peanuts. Get it, Doctor Nightingale? That offer I made to you, which you consider an insult, is the highest weekly wage in this circus."

"You made your point. Now let me make mine. If I agree to your offer, it means essentially I have to abandon my practice for three weeks. And I need an income to replace that because I'm simply not independently wealthy. I work for a living. I have bills to pay. I have a large house and a lot of people who depend on me. It would have been very nice, Mr. Allenbach. I love circuses. I love circus animals. But I simply can't afford your salary."

She walked over to him and extended her hand. He took it. "Why don't you go to the matinee, Doctor Nightingale, and enjoy the show? Think it over. Call me one way or the other after six this evening. Okay?" He gave Didi his card and she walked out.

Once inside the Big Top, Didi spotted her "elves" seated way up in the wooden school-gymnasium-type bleachers that lined both sides of the tent. The four of them looked happy. They were all stuffing themselves with cotton candy or hot dogs or candied apples or popcorn. It was slow going for Didi as she made her way up and through the aisles to join the crew: the stands were now packed with parents and children.

Didi had barely sat down when the lights dimmed and the ringmaster in top hat entered the center of the ring. An all-American brass band started up. Didi looked around. Where was the band? Then she saw a single man in a lighted alcove playing with the controls of a flashing board like the music mixer in a disco. The brass band was canned and computer-generated.

Two clowns ran out into the ring and to the delight of the audience kept interfering with the ringmaster's announcement. Finally it was time for the opening parade. The "band" switched to a version of "Hail to the Chief," and each of the circus stars made his or her appearance, running across the ring and then vanishing out the other side.

First came the Shelty Sisters—five "little people" with the nine Shetland ponies on which they performed their acrobatic feats.

Then came The Great Zappanus in their sequins and capes—the formerly great high-wire artists who now merely performed unbelievable somersaults.

Then the world-famous Lothar Strauss and his three dazzling Bengal tigers, roaring as they were pulled across the ring in their cage.

Finally the fire swallower, Laz Runay—direct! according to the announcer, from the renowned Hungarian State Circus.

The lights went out completely and a hush settled over the crowd. Didi knew what was about to happen. The elephants were coming.

She felt like a six-year-old kid—happy, anticipatory . . . did she love elephants!

"Ladies and gentlemen . . ." the announcer hawked. "From the steaming jungles of Asia, I bring you Tran Van Minh and his beautiful beasts . . . Lutzi and Gorgeous and Alma and Dolly . . . and the great Queen."

A drumroll. A barrage of spotlights and out trotted the first elephant, ridden by the trainer Tran Van Minh. She was a beautiful elephant, bedecked with red and gold trappings.

Behind her marched another awesome beast, this one's trunk holding the first one's tail.

Alma, Dolly, and Queen each carried a dancing girl who began to pirouette wildly the moment her elephant reached the center of the ring. The applause and shouts were deafening.

The elephants pranced out the far side of the tent.

All eyes went back to the center of the ring, where the ringmaster held his enormous whip high in the air.

And then, suddenly, there seemed to be a collective gasp—a kind of astonishment from one part of the bleachers.

Didi turned toward the exit. One of the elephants was backing up into the ring, much to the delight of the audience. The children began to cheer. When she was all the way back, she wheeled suddenly and the dancing girl tumbled off the elephant's back, hitting the ground hard about five feet from her mount.

The elephant ambled over to the little dancer, placed her front foot on the head of the fallen girl, and crushed her to death.

ABOUT THE AUTHOR

Lydia Adamson is the pseudonym of a noted mystery writer who lives in New York.

ENTER THE
MYSTERIOUS WORLD
OF ALICE NESTLETON
IN HER LYDIA
ADAMSON SERIES . . .
BY READING THESE OTHER
PURR-FECT CAT CAPERS
FROM SIGNET

A CAT IN THE MANGER

Alice Nestleton, an off-off Broadway actress turned amateur sleuth, is crazy about cats, particularly her Maine coon, Bushy, and alley cat, Pancho. Alice plans to enjoy a merry little Christmas peacefully cat-sitting at a gorgeous Long Island estate where she expects to be greeted by eight howling Himalayans. Instead she stumbles across a grisly corpse. Alice has unwittingly become part of a deadly game of high-stakes horse racing, sinister seduction, and missing money. Alice knows she'll have to count on her cat-like instincts and (she hopes!) nine lives to solve the murder mystery.

A CAT OF A DIFFERENT COLOR

Alice Nestleton returns home one evening after teaching her acting class at the New School to find a lovestruck student bearing a curious gift—a beautiful white Abyssinian-like cat. The next day the student is murdered in a Manhattan bar, and the rare cat is catnapped! Alice's feline curiosity prompts her to investigate. As the clues unfold, she is led into an underworld of smuggling, blackmail, and murder. Alice sets one of her famous traps to uncover a criminal operation that stretches from downtown Manhattan to South America to the center of New York's diamond district. Alice herself becomes the prey in a cat-and-mouse game before she finds the key to the mystery in a group of unusual cats with an exotic history.

A CAT IN WOLF'S CLOTHING

When two retired city workers are found slain in their apartment, the New York City police discover the same clue that has left them baffled in seventeen murder cases in the past fifteen years—all of the murder victims were cat owners, and a toy was left for each cat at the murder scene. After reaching one too many dead ends, the police decide to consult New York's cagiest crime-solving cat expert, Alice Nestleton. What appears to be the work of one psychotic, cat-loving murderer leads to a tangled web of intrigue as our heroine becomes convinced that the key to the crimes lies in the cats, which mysteriously vanish after the murders. The trail of clues takes Alice from the secretive small towns of the Adirondacks to the eerie caverns beneath Central Park, where she finds that sometimes cat worship can lead to murder.

A CAT BY ANY OTHER NAME

A hot New York summer has Alice Nestleton taking a hiatus from the stage and joining a coterie of cat lovers in cultivating a Manhattan herb garden. When one of the cozy group plunges to her death, Alice is stunned and grief-stricken by the apparent suicide of her close friend. But aided by her two cats, she soon smells a rat. And with the help of her own feline-like instincts, Alice unravels the trail of clues and sets a trap that leads her from the Brooklyn Botanical Gardens right to her own backyard. Could the victim's dearest friends have been her own worst enemies?

A CAT IN THE WINGS

Cats, Christmas, and crime converge when Alice Nestleton finds herself on the prowl for the murderer of a once world-famous ballet dancer. Alice's close friend has been charged with the crime, and it is up to Alice to seek the truth. From Manhattan's meanest streets to the elegant salons of wealthy art patrons, Alice is drawn into a dark and dangerous web of deception, until one very special cat brings Alice the clues she needs to track down the murderer of one of the most imaginative men the ballet world has ever known.

A CAT WITH A FIDDLE

Alice Nestleton's latest job requires her to drive a musician's cat up to rural Massachusetts. The actress, hurt by bad reviews of her latest play, looks forward to a long, restful weekend. But though the woods are beautiful and relaxing, Alice must share the artists' colony with a world-famous quartet beset by rivalries. Her peaceful vacation is shattered when the handsome lady-killer of a pianist turns up murdered. Alice may have a tin ear, but she also has a sharp eye for suspects and a nose for clues. Her investigations lead her from the scenic Berkshire mountains to New York City, but it takes the clue of a rare breed of cats for Alice to piece together the puzzle. Alice has a good idea whodunit, but the local police won't listen, so our intrepid cat lady is soon baiting a dangerous trap for a killer.